WEIRD HORROR MAGAZINE

SPRING 2025

ISSUE 10

Edited by

MICHAEL KELLY

UNDERTOW
PUBLICATIONS

WEIRD HORROR 10
Spring 2025

PUBLISHER
Undertow Publications

EDITOR/LAYOUT
Michael Kelly

PROOFREADER
Carolyn Macdonell

OPINION
Simon Strantzas

COMMENTARY
Orrin Grey

BOOKS
Lysette Stevenson

ART
MK Cooper (cover) and Shikhar Dixit (interior)

COVER DESIGN
Vince Haig

Weirdhorrormagazine.com

Contents

On Horror

Simon Strantzas

Transcendence in Horror

Is positivity antithetical to the horror story? Certainly, there are horror stories with hopeful, uplifting endings where good triumphs over evil (if only temporarily), or where characters at their lowest find the strength to go on and continue to fight even when common sense tells them it's fruitless. But in many of these cases, what serves as positivity is divorced from the horror. By which I mean the horrific aspect of the story remains inherently pessimistic, and it's only through a reaction to (or the rejection of) that horror that the positive outcome is attained.

But can the horror *itself* be positive? We typically view horror through a negative lens—bad things happening to good people, bad things happening to bad people, bad things simply happening —and though weird fiction does introduce a handful of variations (where we might describe the horror as bad, though not necessarily evil), the truth is what makes something a horror story is inextricably linked to this negative perspective. Horror fiction is fiction viewed through the prism of the bad. Or, at the very least, of the dark. And, for most, fiction written and read this way is inherently read as pessimistic. That's the crux of its appeal.

After all, we are positing that the unknown that is invading reality (whether from without or from within) is a threat to the status quo, and the implicit suggestion is that the status quo is good; therefore, anything that threatens it is bad. The ghost in the painting, the creature under the rectory, the ancient god in outer space...they all want to upset the normal with the abnormal. All of this is bad. All of this suggests that, even in otherwise uplifting stories, the notion of horror itself is not.

Which returns us to the question: can horror be positive? Can it be hopeful? And if so, how?

The most obvious avenue is via religious transcendence.

Though I'm talking about lowercase-r "religious", it as easily applies to uppercase-R "Religious" as well. Russell Kirk, in addition to his conservative writings, penned ghost stories. And while he wrote comparatively few of them, they still rank highly among readers steeped in the subgenre—the most famous being his short story: "There's a Long Long Trail A-Winding". What Kirk brought to the ghost story—and by extension the horror story—was in the introduction of religious thought, not as a method of opposing horror but as an aspect of horror itself. By this I don't mean he demonized or perverted religion—his stories were markedly not anti-religious. Instead, they celebrated religion and religious transcendence and depicted their power as a result of, not in spite of, the horror.

The work of poet, author, and musician Nick Cave similarly illustrates religious transcendence through his work. While Cave readily admits that religion plays a part in his life, he does not approach it with blind faith, but rather as a skeptic looking for something more; something ineffable that operates beyond our understanding while also being essential to life. Many of his songs explore this interstitial reach for the unknown, and he excels at portraying moments of catharsis and transcendence, perhaps nowhere as breathtakingly as when he proclaims that there is a war coming in "Hiding it All Away". This translates easily to horror when we understand that the ineffable is merely the unknowable Other in different clothing, and the intrusion of the divine into the day-to-day can only be unsettling or horrifying to those who don't understand what they're experiencing.

Or, to put it another way: stories of transformation and transcendence, even when depicted in a positive light, are by their nature horror stories, because the act of transforming, of transcending, is both painful and frightening. And yet, they are implicitly positive and uplifting when one recognizes that transcending suggests reaching a better state than one was in before. An arguably happier state.

Both horror and happiness are subjective concepts. They mean different things to different people, and we can tell stories that are horrific from the reader's perspective while being the opposite from the character's. Films such as *Midsommar* or *Saint Maude* may be examples of this positive horror—each ends with their protagonist experiencing a horrific moment that simultaneously evokes a feeling of dread in the viewer, while also depicting a character going through a profoundly freeing and uplifting experience. One where the horror has uplifted them from unhappiness to something more divine. In short: they have transcended.

One of the most affecting examples of transcendence in horror that I've read in recent years is Janaka Stucky's long poem *Ascend Ascend*. Written during a trance state, it portrays a kabbalistic ascent and does so using the forms and language of horror. Dark imagery and grotesqueries are used to portray the narrator's state of mind and view of the world. These horrific images of death and mortality are the places from which we, as readers, climb, ascending further from the physical into the spiritual, culminating in a transcendence that is at once beautiful and terrifying. I'm hard-pressed to think of a more affecting piece of work, or better example of the ideas I've attempted to outline in this column.

Horror is often pigeonholed into specific boxes, its walls defined by those aspects that are most common and, often, most trite. The horror genre is not alone in this, of course—humanity's nature is to find patterns and commonalities and group things accordingly—but as much as that evolutionarily has helped us, it can also allow us to overlook the nuances of things. In this case, how powerful and versatile speculative fiction through a dark lens can be. Horror is, of course, about how all love will end, how all lovers will die, how all plans will fail, how nothing will survive; but it can also be about how we deal with adversity and our fears and pains and not just persevere but how we can rise above them and be changed by them.

Fiction about transcendence through horror is necessarily

fiction about change and metamorphosis. About one's true self being revealed. About how we can be made not only better but be made new by our most troubling, painful experiences. This is an important lesson, and it only grows more important every day. Horror delivers this positive message to us if only we'll allow ourselves to listen. If only we'll let go of who we once were and prepare to become something more.

Grey's Grotesqueries

Orrin Grey

Weird Little Guys: Gargoyles, Grotesques, and Monster Toys

WE ALL LOVE weird little guys.

From gargoyles to those weirdos in the marginalia of illuminated manuscripts, they have been with us for about as long as people have been visually representing things from their imaginations. A popular account on Twitter and now on Bluesky is dedicated exclusively to sharing "weird medieval guys," from heraldic beasts to the anthropomorphic animals, demons, and other oddities drawn by monks on illuminated manuscripts of all kinds.

What defines a weird little guy, as distinct from any other monster? To some extent, you just know them when you see them, and in the hands of the right artist even a titanic kaiju like Godzilla can be a weird little guy. Usually, though, weird little guys are about what you'd expect from the name:

They're little, often smaller than a person. They're weird—if they're something that exists in the real world at all, then they're probably altered in some way, like rabbits walking on their hind legs and using tools. And they're usually at least a little bit anthropomorphized. They may not fully be wearing clothes, speaking a recognizable language, or anything like that, but they're often at least a little bit person-like.

From leering on the sides of churches to getting up to whatever they get up to in the margins of medieval manuscripts, weird little guys have made their way into all manner of media over the years. You can find them all over the place in movies, of course, where they attain perhaps their ultimate expression in Joe Dante's *Gremlins*, the eponymous "mean-spirited, gloppy little monsters" being peak weird little guys.

In fact, the *idea* of the gremlin is pretty illustrative of weird little guys as a whole. A kind of cryptid of the industrial age, gremlins were first popularized by pilots in the early part of the 20th century as a way to explain malfunctions in aircraft, becoming particularly widespread during World War II.

From there, gremlins spread out to explain breakdowns in all sorts of mechanical devices. Before Joe Dante's film, gremlins had already appeared in Bugs Bunny cartoons, a Roald Dahl novel, and, memorably, in the *Twilight Zone* episode "Nightmare at 20,000 Feet," adapted from Richard Matheson's 1961 short story of the same name.

While the specifics of gremlins vary from source to source, they are pretty much always weird little guys. Anthropomorphic but certainly not human, they delight in causing mischief. "Gremlins think it's fun to hurt you," warns one of many World War II-era industrial safety posters that cautioned people about the menace.

Though only sometimes directly antagonistic, weird little guys like gremlins can be quite dangerous, yet we have a certain fondness for them nevertheless. This manifests in a variety of media where weird little guys are heroes rather than villains—without necessarily losing that essential weirdness.

One of my favorite examples from the 21st century is the aggressively merchandized little blue alien from *Lilo & Stitch*. Though Stitch ultimately locates his place among a found family, his "destructive programming" and often uncouth behavior makes him unmistakably a weird little guy. (It doesn't hurt that he is also little, and anthropomorphized.)

I think we have probably always had an affection for these weird little guys. There's a reason why people carved them into the stonework of churches, or took great pains to draw them in the margins of manuscripts. Today, this is represented partly by artists who continue to create weird little guys wherever they can, but also in our desire to purchase weird little (albeit inanimate) guys of our own.

Funko Pops are among the most popular collectibles in the world right now, occupying a spot that was once the purview of Beanie Babies, and many of them could certainly qualify as weird little guys. And I've already mentioned how heavily merchandized characters like Stitch are.

Leaving aside the immediate collectability of familiar characters from pop culture, however, there are types of toys that are basically just weird little guy factories, and always have been. Several of these originate in Japan, particularly the various lines of soft vinyl or "sofubi" figures, which often depict kaiju of various stripes, and the so-called keshi figures, whose best-known iteration might be the M.U.S.C.L.E. men that were popular in the '80s—an acronym short for "Millions of Unusual Small Creatures Lurking Everywhere," a description of weird little guys if ever there was one.

Even the popular cheap monster finger puppets that are sometimes available as Halloween giveaways or from vending machines are ideal examples of weird little guys.

Within the realm of sofubi and keshi collecting, makers have staked out a spot designing and releasing often limited runs of odd creatures of their own design, making what was heretofore a largely industrialized and commodified operation into something much more specialized and bespoke and, as a result, weirder and littler. Those who collect these monster toys have particular artists that they follow, and some sofubi figures, in particular, can fetch prices commensurate to fine art pieces.

Admittedly, most of the people I know are nerds of one stripe or another, and many of them are writers, artists, game designers, and so on, frequently in the horror spectrum. Yet I still think it says something about the abiding appeal of weird little guys that virtually every person I know has at least a few toys, figures, gaming miniatures, and so on that would fit the bill lurking around somewhere in their office or studio, fulfilling a role similar to those leering gargoyles from so many centuries ago.

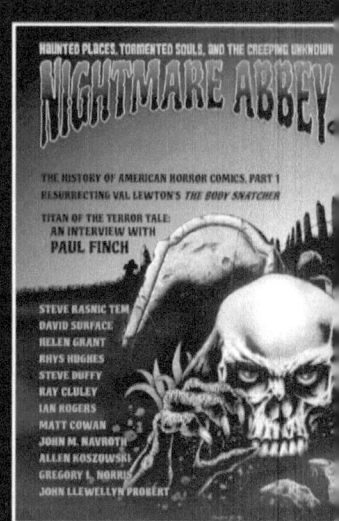

St. Dymphna's School for Borderland Girls

Jocelyn Szczepaniak-Gillece

THE FIRST GIRL was found prone in front of the altar, her arms out to each side mimicking the sign of the cross. "Prostrate," the proper term, guaranteed to evoke a stifled giggle with its vulgar reference point. "Vulgar," another one. Dirty words were not to be spoken and so their compatriots had to be identified: words a letter or two off, words that hid their mysteries until the tongue tied up.

That was one of the first lessons the girls all learned: anything could be dirty if you looked from the right angle.

At first they thought she might have just been genuflecting on her way between bells, then caught the spirit and plummeted face-first in passion. That happened sometimes, though mostly with the girls everyone knew were convent-bound. But this was Michelle, who was not nun material. She was lucky she hadn't gotten pregnant. Who knows, though, maybe she had and just dug out the embryo with an empty hanger typically used to air out a uniform shirt in need of washing. No one would be the wiser as long as she aimed right. Stranger things had happened at St. Dymphna's School for Borderland Girls.

Michelle was not, as it turned out, channeling the almighty presence of the Lord. Michelle was unconscious with her eyes wide open and her body rigid, the only part of her in motion the rippling back and forth of the moist tongue that lolled out of her mouth. Michelle, the sisters said, was high on some sort of contraband. Michelle would be in the infirmary for the foreseeable future. And then Michelle would be sent home.

None of this made any sort of sense. No one received any care packages anymore, let alone secret deliveries of forbidden pharmaceuticals from longing admirers. The infirmary had long since run out of any medication beyond dusty half-full containers of Midol, which everyone knew did nothing for menstrual pain. And no one had heard from their parents in weeks, or maybe months; it was hard to tell when everyday was Sunday.

After the priest stopped showing up once a week, the girls had rejoiced at the potential reprieve. Instead, the meetings for prayer just increased, as though a community in chorus might stave off whatever threats had slowly and effectively shut the school off from the rest of the world. Whatever was out there, it growled sometimes, past the manicured courtyard with its neoclassical sculptures and hedge rows, past the border of the school grounds where the dark and lonely forest began.

But Michelle went to the infirmary anyway and all the girls went to their classes as before and, as had become normal, to prayer several times a day.

When evil is afoot in the world, one must don one's oxygen mask and then place masks over the faces of the younger ones. Lift every voice and sing.

In more usual days, Michelle's roommate Alma might have been destined for the nunnery after graduation. Small and nervous, glasses, voice like a mouse, Alma wasn't much of a confidante for her worldlier companion, and so they kept to themselves, sharing little more than a late-night snack or conditioner when the other ran out.

That didn't mean, however, that Alma hadn't seen what Michelle was doing late at night.

Alma had a few useful gifts but good sleep was not among them. She woke multiple times most nights. It was the way things were and she accepted it as she had her first communion wafer, which was at the time far too large and rough-edged for her delicate little seven-year-old mouth. The wafer's relief cross was a scabbard trying to close over the sword of her tongue. But she swallowed it anyway and tried to let her sense of accomplishment flow like cool water and wash the Jesus down her throat.

Accomplishment became an addiction akin to what Alma imagined others experienced from religious fervor. The return of a perfect test. The well-risen cake removed at the exact turn from sludgy to baked. The room tidied from hurricane to sanctuary. None of it the passion of doing something, but rather the satisfaction of something having been done.

Michelle, what a difference: an acolyte of the half-completed. Lacy bras hanging from the desk chair. Alarms snoozed in multiples every morning. Sticks of gum split down the middle, half chewed passionately to saliva-drenched silky putty between pearlescent teeth and half left to harden on the desktop in the exposed air. Michelle didn't even finish a meal; she mixed everything on her plate like a heathen and left most of it to congeal in a sodden mass as she snuck off for a cigarette.

That was why, the first time it happened, Alma thought maybe Michelle was sleepwalking while hungry.

Alma woke around 3 a.m. as she usually did, but it was from a noise. Something slurping and repetitive. She opened her eyes. A thin band of moonlight sluiced through the curtain and dribbled down in silver shards on the floor. Michelle was not in bed and, no surprise, the sheets were in total disarray. Alma looked blearily around the room for anything else out of the ordinary. And then she found it.

Michelle knelt in the moonlight, knees and face right up against the wall. The back of her cotton nightgown was soaked in sweat. Her head moved up and down rhythmically. Her hands splayed out onto the wall, keeping her upright, as her head bobbed.

A not-altogether-unfamiliar and not-altogether-unwanted sensation slinked through Alma's lower half. She crept down the bed to get a better glimpse.

Michelle's eyes were squeezed shut, though not in agony but in sustained and intense pleasure. Her nose was scraped and bloody at the tip from rubbing. Her tongue was stuck out of her mouth as far as it would go and licked up and down the same spot on the wall. There was, Alma could just barely see in the moonlight, a long dark ribbon streaming from a crack in the wall right above Michelle's brow: a thin flood of viscous fluid, crimson, bloody.

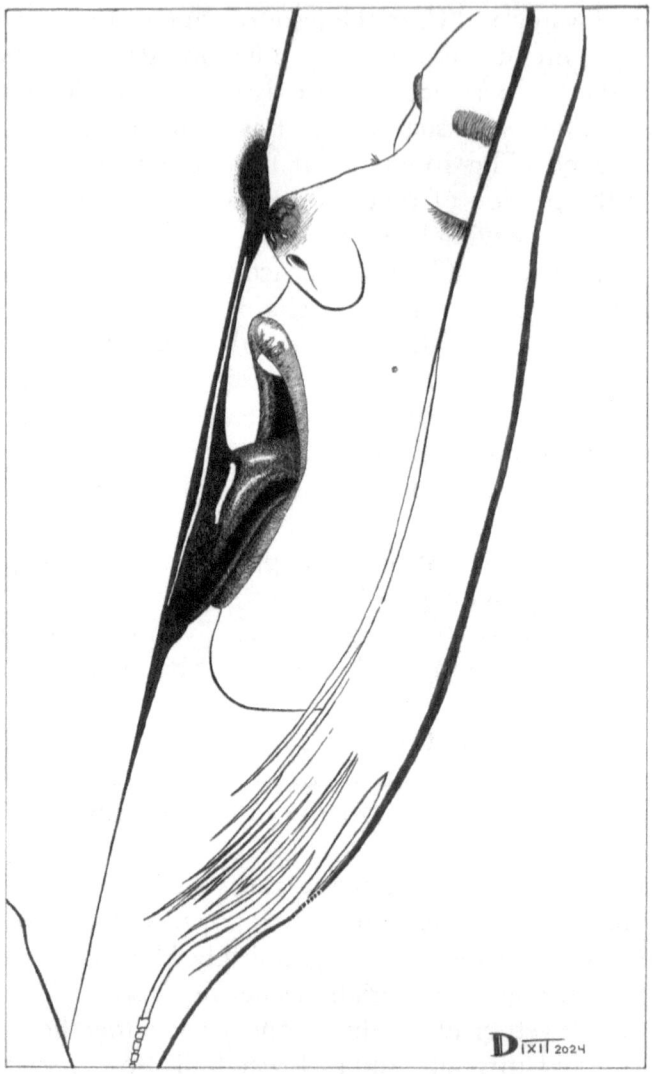

Alma croaked out her roommate's name, but Michelle didn't budge, just kept licking and licking, and now her tongue was bruised and swollen from the nubby old plaster, now she was getting down past the first layer of paint, and still the fluid trickled from the crack. Now her tongue was ragged and purple, now the fluid had stained all around her mouth, now her lips were flaking and bloody, "Michelle," Alma cried, but nothing, nothing but the licking, any other time a small noise, but in the silence of the dead of night a sound like boulders scraping against cavern entrances to let the murderers in.

Alma crawled deep under the covers and didn't come out from under them until morning.

◠

DESPITE THE FACT that Alma woke every night to the same scene, Michelle still seemed normal for a week or so, as normal as anyone was now that the world outside St. Dymphna's had all but vanished.

Everyone had already been used to shutting out the world to better hear the word of God anyway, so when the food deliveries slowed and then ceased it didn't feel quite as terrifying as it might have at a secular school. There was a plentiful garden in the summer and preserves stashed in the basement for winter. Beehives for honey.

And so Michelle's sharpness in the eye and edge in the voice could be explained away as maybe just a girl who always wanted to escape, realizing that the ways out had all caved in. Maybe her shrillness was just that of an animal cornered.

Alma was privy to the nighttime secrets, and so when her roommate was found in a state of holy rapture, at first she wanted to correct them in the hopes a new treatment might be sought out to rouse Michelle from her uncanny coma.

But speaking up didn't come easy to Alma. And when she thought more about it, telling on Michelle might lead Alma to tell on her own feelings that arose when she watched her roommate ecstatically lick the walls. And when she thought more about that, it made her turn toward confession. And when she thought more about that, her tongue got tied like a maraschino cherry stem.

And so Alma stayed quiet.

◠

THE SECOND GIRL appeared in the foyer under the marble holy water font as though she had been crawling on the floor like one possessed and banged her head against the stone. Like Michelle, Penelope was splayed out in the shape of the cross, her face pressed hard against the floor, unresponsive to touch, a slap. Like Michelle, Penelope was taken to the infirmary and placed under surveillance until whatever she'd taken could wear off.

The other girls clustered around as the strongest of the sisters lifted Penelope up under her arms and her satin nightgown strap slipped down her shoulder. Alma watched the jostling reveal the delicate curve of the unconscious girl's breast, the graceful arch of her hip, the outline of her hourglass waist looking like a perfect fit for a searching hand.

Alma sat by herself at dinner that evening, as she had since Michelle's illness. She gazed into her meager food and measured the visual weight of Penelope's soft body against her memory of Michelle's.

"I saw her doing it."

A hiss from a sidling body startled Alma from her reverie. Smooth as a worm, another girl had slipped into the seat next to her: Gerry with her constantly overfilling eyes, her constantly running nose, her skin tinged green with constant viruses running roughshod over her weak immune system. Gerry, Penelope's roommate.

"Every night. Like clockwork. Up against the wall with her tongue. Her mouth. I thought she was going to get me sick. But she got sick."

Gerry sneezed and a trail of snot, limacine and glutinous, dangled from one nostril. Alma stared at it, entranced by its glistening amorphousness.

"Claire told me it's happening in her room, too. Sharon's up to it, sucking up that stuff like a wine cooler through a straw. So who else? Michelle must've done it. Did you see her? I'll take your silence for agreement."

Alma nodded. There was no place for anything but acquiescence with this one. And anyway, there was something happening.

"Might as well try to piece it together, right? Might as well cooperate on this. Here."

Gerry grabbed for Alma's hand. Her annelid fingers pressed a key, clammy with sweat, into Alma's palm.

"It's for Claire's room. She told me to come by late tonight. I told her I'd talk to you. You have the key now; you have to show up. Let's go see if it's the same thing in there. And who knows? Even if it's not, we might get a glimpse of something naughty. Don't tell sister."

Gerry grinned wetly, her canines her only formed and sharp features.

"See you in the hall at midnight-oh-five."

~

ALMA DIDN'T FALL asleep until 11 p.m., then jolted awake an hour later. Pocketing the key from her nightstand, she crept into the hall-way. Little drips of moonlight the color of Gerry's snot spilled from the transoms onto the dark oak floors.

Gerry slid out from a door as though summoned.

"You brought it, right?" she whispered. "Let's go."

Alma tried to keep up with Gerry as she nestled her sea snake body from shadow to shadow, but she kept losing sight of her. Then Gerry would smile at her and the greenish moonlight reflected off her spittle and Alma started following her again. They came to a stop in front of a door toward the end of the southern hallway.

"Pass it over," Gerry hissed, and Alma handed her the key.

The room was uncanny in its moonlit black-and-white familiar-ity, as though Alma's room had been sent through a Xerox machine. The same two twin beds, the same brass crucifixes hanging above the same pillows, the same wooden desks, the same single window.

But that was all to be expected here at St. Dymphna's. They were meant to be copies of one another, at least to the extent possible given their different skin tones and hair colors and heights, at least in terms of the purity of what lay between their adolescent ears. What was truly disturbing for Alma and perhaps even Gerry was the repetition of what had happened to their roommates.

Claire sat underneath the window, her little feet tucked up under her nightgown, her eyes wide and her pale blonde hair stringy around her ears. She acknowledged the other girls with a "shhh!" and quick shuffling in place as they sat next to her and turned to face the eastern wall.

Beautiful vicious Sharon knelt there, eyes closed in rapture, tongue sticking out like Kali, resting forward on her hands propped in front of her. Drips of a liquid the viscosity of maple syrup and the color of rusted pipes drizzled down the wall to her open mouth where she sucked it up like a milkshake. Sharon, five foot one, her nails painted bitch pink, the heels of her feet forever baby soft like her deodorant, always looking like she was about to be tossed up in the air and caught by a waiting suitor, here transformed into just a greedy little mouth seeking a devilish sacrament.

"She's been at it since around eleven," Claire whispered. "It'll probably go on until almost dawn."

The three of them sat, hypnotized, for hours, the only sound Sharon's tongue lapping up wall liquid like a cat at a saucer. When she finally ceased as the sky turned lavender, she turned from the wall, her eyes shut, the tip of her adorable nose bruised and raw, her rosebud lips scabby and coated, and staggered into bed.

"Show's over," Claire shrugged. "Watch it while you can. I know she'll be next."

Delirium settled over Alma's brain as she lay in her room, alone. In the brief moments of sleep before the bells woke her again, she dreamt of Michelle, Penelope, and Sharon on the school lawn forming a human pyramid with Sharon at the top. When Sharon jumped from her perch and somersaulted three times in the air, the girls all screamed in joy. The sky darkened and the clouds fell and the ground opened up and flames licked the yawning chasm from below and the girls all tumbled in shrieking in terrible pain and horrible pleasure and Alma woke, trembling, and went to breakfast.

～

CLAIRE, of course, was right. Just two days later, Sharon was found in the kitchen, eyes rolled back in her head, stiff like a corpse. Both panic and thrill set in among the girls.

The last time the newspapers had arrived, there was warning of invasion and terror. And now here they were, alone, no deliveries, but enough to sustain them for the time being, however long that might be.

The woods around the school, though, seemed darker and more forbidding and emitted regular sounds like jaws snapping or a symphony of stomachs digesting. No one went walking on the hiking trails anymore; they stayed in the walled gardens. Even the track team practiced by running up and down the long driveway.

The world around them was closing in but it all felt very boring. As long as they didn't get too close to the forest's border of wicked branches, the girls felt utterly, frustratingly safe. Security muffled their days into one long interminable one. At least if the devastation reached St. Dymphna's, at least something would happen.

But at last something was happening, much as the sisters tried to confine it. Girls were changing. And predictions were made as to who was next.

It wasn't too difficult to see that the lord of hysteria was choosing the most beautiful for his brides. Like most of her allotment in life, Alma found this categorically unfair; now her mousiness not only stopped any first kisses before they could happen, now it kept her from experiencing the most exciting thing to ever happen at St. Dymphna's.

Still, she wasn't sure she even wanted it. After all, from being among the first to see the secrets, Alma was granted a front-row seat at the other transformations. And that in itself was a thrill.

Night after night, girls asked Gerry to come to their rooms to see if what they were witnessing was the same that had happened to Penelope. And night after night, Gerry dragged Alma to another room to sit and watch the madness unfold.

Gerry began taking notes in a discarded journal printed with unicorns another girl gave her and examined the similarities between cases: measuring the distance from the wall and the wall licker, the time of night it started, how long before she suffered the seizure and settled into stasis. Comparing one case to another gave her an air of the inspector, such that the other girls began to talk to her rather than turning up their noses at her sluggish appearance. It was good for Gerry, Alma figured. She needed it.

But Alma relished the watching. That's all, just the watching. The beautiful teenage girl, the wall, the unbridled desire. Satisfying in some way both banal and profound, whatever that way was. It gave her insight into all those movies she wasn't supposed to watch made by Italian men decades older than her. Is this what they were after, she thought. Well, I'm starting to see it now. I get the appeal.

Things hit their own kind of stasis: the licking, the hours, the disappearance, the next one, the prayers and the schoolwork during the day, the waiting to watch at night. That is, until the sisters left.

~

SISTER ROBERTA ANNOUNCED at breakfast that the infirmary was full. "We have no more cots," she said. "We have no medicine. Someone needs to go for help."

"I'm going to raise my hand," Gerry whispered to Alma.

Before Alma had a chance to respond, Sister Roberta spoke again. "And no, none of the students are going. I will. This afternoon."

"Bitch," Gerry hissed and rubbed her slimy nose with the back of her hand. Alma let out a held breath.

The students clustered around the doors at Sister Roberta's departure time and stared as she waddled determinedly down the driveway with her leather doctor's bag. She reached the tree border, thickened with vines, and turned around, a bright white smudge against the darkness. All the girls waved at her and she turned back toward the forest, hacking at the brush with an umbrella. Just like that, she was in it, and the nun-shaped hole she'd made closed up almost instantaneously like a gulping mouth. And then she was gone.

That night, Alma and Gerry had three potential viewing options.

"Why choose?" Gerry said. "We've got all night."

They spent two hours observing Stacey, two hours with Allison, and Alma hurried them along for the three hours before dawn with Kristen. She'd always given Alma a nasty side-eye through her perfect curtain of shiny brown hair, brandishing her field hockey stick like a weapon. But seeing her like this, up against the wall, for the first time Alma felt a warm kinship, recognized the beauty in her razor features and tight tendons.

It only made sense that Kristen must be beautiful, because

she'd been chosen. Letting that into her heart gave Alma a sense of beneficence and watching her on her knees gave her the sweet enjoyment of being catered to by an underling. Three hours was barely enough.

And the next day, all three of them were in stasis.

The other sisters tried to find out-of-the-way spots for the frozen beauties, but all that was left were recliners and Adirondacks. So Stacey and Allison were placed on easy chairs by the fireplace while Kristen was positioned on the lawn like she was sunbathing or waiting her turn to enter a match. The sisters covered her with a blanket after the sunset, and while they pledged to watch her all night, Sister Anita fell asleep while keeping guard.

In the morning, Kristen was gone, the only trace of her a path where her body was dragged from the chair to the forest. Sister Anita screamed and ran pell-mell into the woods, which closed around her with a thunderous rumble. With that, tensions rose.

The remaining five sisters elected two more to enter the forest. The decision was made quickly and with little discussion, almost as though Sister Edna and Sister Cecilia wanted to go. Like Sister Roberta, they were swallowed up immediately, nothing left to be seen.

Worse still, the girls in stasis followed Kristen, though no one witnessed them getting up and leaving. Three more gone by the next morning, three footpaths worn down in the overgrown grass ending at the woods. Sister Blanche walked down one path with a magnifying glass, intending to stop before the trees, but as she got to the thorns she just kept going, bent half over and staring through the glass, until she could be seen no more.

The rest of the girls in stasis were soon gone, too, their only sign the flattened grass where they crawled—or were pulled—to the forest.

By now, Alma realized, there were no beautiful girls left, only their roommates. What was next?

~

Two DAYS LATER, Claire was in stasis.

"She tried it," Gerry reported. "She told me she was going to. She tried it and look where she is now."

Alma looked over at where Claire lay at the base of the steps, twitching a bit. Besides her malady, Claire looked different. Lusher hair, less stringy. A glow to her cheeks. Prettier, even. Her lips reddened with rusty fluid. Alma had never thought she would care to watch Claire lick the wall, but remorse crept in at the notion that now she never would.

The two sisters left, Sister Jean and Sister Frances, shuffled around with haunted eyes and served porridge at every meal. Alma could barely watch Gerry shoveling it into her mouth, the soft salted grains ringing her wet lips and thickening her spit when she talked.

"Aren't you sick of it?" Gerry asked. "It tastes like nothing. Don't you wish you had something richer?"

The implication hung in the air between them, heavy and damp.

"I do," Gerry said. "I'm hungry."

Though the windows were closed, Alma could sense the deepening guttural roar of the forest underlying the courtyard's hesitant hush.

It didn't matter that no one saw Sister Jean and Sister Frances leave, nor did their departure really affect anyone's moods. Once all the sisters had gone into the woods, the remaining girls scrounged up what they could in the kitchen for breakfasts of bouillon and anchovies.

Alma took advantage of the opportunity to satisfy her curiosity by digging through the sisters' dressers, but all she found were scapulars and calendars. The mystery of their lives, it turned out, was simply that they had chosen them at all.

Fewer and fewer girls came to eat. Alma didn't need to walk into their rooms at night to know what they were doing. It was, after all, the only thing left, whether she liked it or not.

When the girls gathered in the evenings by the fire, their eyes glistened like champagne flutes. They barely spoke to one another, but when one caught another's eye they smiled languidly and cast their gazes upward as though admiring some cosmic phenomenon.

Alma tried to read in the evening but when she least expected it a girl would shout "Ah! Did you see that?" Everyone would turn toward where she gestured and gasp with wonder. Alma, too, would turn but nothing was ever there, just the shadows deepening at the edge of the curtains.

Even Gerry faded quicker from Alma's understanding. Her flesh grew tighter and less aqueous, her eyes more limpid, her gait more graceful than slithery.

"You know what I'm doing," she said to Alma. "Don't you want to watch?"

Alma found that, to her surprise, she did.

That night she crept by herself down the hallway to Gerry's door where she turned the knob without knocking. Moonlight poured in through the window like milk from a glass. Gerry knelt against the wall, but where once the wall bore a trickle of liquid, now it was a forceful stream, splashing against her cheeks and chin, dribbling down her chest and soaking her gown.

"Gerry," Alma said, realizing that she had never thought to speak to one of the girls under the sacramental hypnosis. "Gerry. Geraldine. What does it feel like?"

Gerry turned, her eyes pressed shut in ecstasy.

"Like knowledge flowing into me, like revelation turning my flesh inside out. Explosive, like a comet. Like there's something within me now and it's searching all my deepest corners for a way to get out."

She licked all across her lips, which were rouged and raw. Her newly thick and dusky eyelashes brushed her cheeks, drips of fluid caught in them glimmering like rubies in a reliquary.

"It's simple, really. I don't want this body anymore," Gerry said. "Does anyone? Let's turn toward transcendence."

Gerry grabbed for Alma's hand to guide her down next to her, but Alma shook it off and ran into the hallway. Back in her room, the holy blood cascaded down her wall in a torrent, begging her to sip from the cup, but she huddled under the blanket and wished the voices away as best she could.

So IT WAS that every other girl went into stasis and disappeared until Alma was the only student left in St. Dymphna's. But it was, she knew, only a matter of time until she succumbed.

The woods were bolder, the noises louder. At night, she could hear Gerry's voice, or what passed for it, whispering outside her window, inviting her to drink. Sometimes it sounded like Michelle was with her, which was strange since they never acknowledged one another before. We're all friends now, they answered. We share in the sanctified knowledge. We even share our bodies.

The forest giggled. And then it screamed.

Every wall in St. Dymphna's began to leak blood. Alma couldn't go anywhere without the temptation surrounding her: day, night, afternoon, it begged of her to taste, just a bit, just see if you like it.

Alma wished she wanted it more. But what she really wanted was to watch it happen. Above all other desire was that of witness.

There was no sense in staying. There was not a dry spot in the school. St. Dymphna's was a bathtub of blood, which was, Alma knew, what came from the walls. Human or otherwise, it splashed around her feet anywhere she went. And the liquid itself whispered to her in secret languages that she almost comprehended. The longer she listened the more fluent she became.

When she understood what the fluid was telling her, Alma took off her clothes and bathed in the blood, letting it cover her until she resembled both a flayed body and a scarlet empress. She walked outside to the middle of the courtyard.

Wildflowers turned toward the sky, their colors changed from yellow and white to livid carmine and vulgar fuchsia and other glaring hues Alma didn't recognize. Sparkling auras wheeled around every blossom, every leaf. Moonlight dappled the ground, turning the grassy hills into the rippling hide of a mighty horse. The nude statues revolved toward her as she passed, the tips of their breasts sharpened to points, their hair swaying like snakes, their smiles widening and new teeth showing.

Alma turned to look at the school for a final time. St. Dymphna's stood out against the charred sky as though spotlit on a stage. In the limelight, it was incongruous with its surroundings: a white stone edifice carved out of thickened space like the design on a coin. But also like the design on a coin, it was not entirely there; its dimensionality was off, making it seem less like a building and more like a representation of one, as though if Alma walked around the back it would prove to be flat like a paper doll with tabs bent to help it stand up.

There was no going back inside because it had no inside anymore. Soon, Alma thought, neither would she.

Ululations rose from the forest.

Shapes formed in the shadows of the trees in the general outlines of bodies. But then the shape would twist like a dress on a clothesline and one limb would turn to three or only a half, a head would turn to a chest, an outstretched hand to an eyelid, a mouth to an organ on the outside of a body.

The shapes took on a bit more solidity, a waxen slick weightiness like the foot of a snail. They organized and reorganized themselves into fractal iterations, bending and abstracting and solving themselves into equations of flesh. Each one bled into the next and then separated again, then met the other and melded seamlessly into a single pinkish wave the color of a manicured fingernail.

"It's you," the bodies murmured. "It's us. Come and see. Come and see."

Alma thrummed like a tuning fork with a deep and hellish tone and the reverberations shook everything solid into air. Behind Alma, the school winked out. But she had already forgotten it ever existed. Her vision exploded into kaleidoscopic signals where infinite forms met one another and split off again.

Out on the border, the land and everything on it disintegrated into vibration.

In the Dream, He is Skinless and Beautiful

Spencer Nitkey

IT'S NOT A DREAM, but it feels like one. Trite checks by dragging the point of his pocket knife across the skin of his stomach. He carves a snowflake shape, six equidistant lines out from a joined center, each ending in small mirrored branches. The skin turns to raised, red ridges, and he enjoys the topography of himself for a moment before turning back to the classroom around him.

A projector plays grainy footage of World War I soldiers dying in trenches in the dimness, so he pricks the center of the snowflake to be sure. A needle-point of blood pricks out from the skin. He sighs and stops himself from more. In a dream, his skin would fall from his body like dandruff, whole sheets as thin as mandolined zucchinis.

Once, when he was very small, there was a hollow tree in his backyard. If he wedged himself inside the small circular opening just a few feet off the ground, he could chimney his way up to the top of the tree, where the dead branches opened like a crown and he could peer out at the whole neighborhood. His father cut the tree down four nights after his thirteenth birthday, so a storm would not send it splintering into their home. Trite just watched from his window, certain he would not know what it was to be held that tightly ever again.

Class ends, and he would like to stay still for a while longer, but he can't. He's pushed, like a luge, through the hallways with the kind of mindless momentum that comes in large groups of people. He spends his next period of the day practicing the grounding technique his therapist taught him a month ago. Five things he can see. Four things he can touch. Three things he can hear. Two things he can smell. One thing he can taste. Over and over and over again until the sewing machine pace of his heart subsides and he can hear anything other than ringing and the sound of his stifled hyperventilation. He's pretty sure he's sweating in the back of Ms. Eckerson's class while she defines entropy on the board and writes out long equations.

Soon there is nothing left to taste, so he turns to his cuticles. He runs their roughed, unhealed terrain along his lips. The desire to flay himself swells like a red tide just behind his throat until he relents.

He catches a small thread of himself between his teeth and pulls. The thin line of skin goes easily, like a poorly sewn sweater, until it lifts, just behind his finger nail. He does not swallow his skin but places it between his fingers and rolls it until it is the texture of putty.

He finds each divot and imperfection on each of his cuticles and either picks or bites at them until most of his fingers are bleeding. He hides his hands in his pockets and asks to use the restroom. His teacher looks annoyed until she sees who it was who asked and her face flashes with pity for a moment, that acrid look like someone biting into a too-salted meal someone they love has made them.

He speed-walks out of the school's front door and sits in his driver's seat in the parking lot. He doesn't cry but he thinks if he could it would help sort things out a little. It's not a dream, but he's beginning to wish it was one. In middle-school his best-friend Tyler once told him that when he turned sixteen, he would steal a handle of vodka from his parents' liquor cabinet, drive three miles down dirt roads into the woods until he found the Carranza memorial and drink as much as he could, just once, to experience what it felt to be really, truly, helpless.

When Trite's hands finally stop shaking he puts the car into drive and speeds until he hits the tree line. Tall, impossibly frail looking pines stand in a row. He creeps his car along until he finds the small dirt road and drives into the woods.

In 1928 a Mexican pilot, Emilio Carranza, who had successfully flown from Mexico to New York was flying back home when his small plane crashed in the middle of the New Jersey pine barrens. The Mexican government paid for a twelve-foot stone monument to be erected at the crash site. They never built anything around it. Instead, it stands, a strange clearing in the otherwise middle of the woods. In the autumnal midday, Trite pulls his car close to the monument and sits outside, laying with his back on the hood, wishing it was cold enough for his breath to fog.

The tree-dappled light is too dreamlike. On one side of the memorial's four faces they carved an arrow pointing to the sky. He takes his pocket knife out of his backpack and runs it along his arm. He places his right hand across his chest to pull the skin taut, holds the knife in his left hand and slices an outline of the arrow on the memorial onto his chest. He draws blood this time, just a little, as he presses. He pulls the knife away and confirms he is bleeding.

Ever since Tyler died, he spends most nights dreaming of shedding his skin like moose antlers. In the dream, it all comes off in one smooth sheet. In reality, he knows his body clings to its skin much harder than that. Still.

At the edge of the clearing in the middle of the woods, where the trees begin to retake what's theirs, Trite notices a pair of boots spread a stride's length from one another. They are pointing into the thicket of trees and he goes closer to look at them because he has not been interested in anything for a long time. When he reaches them he sees footprints in the mud leading away from them, deeper into the trees.

He looks back at his car, which seems smeared. It's not a dream, but he wants it to be. He walks into the pine barrens, following the direction of the boots. He finds bare-footprints in the just-dried mud behind the tree line. Good, then. He has a direction. He worries he will lose his way back if it rains, or the wind blows too hard, or he cannot find the footprints again.

It would not be so bad, he thinks, to become lost in the woods, if one is to become lost anywhere. He would not like to become lost in a dream, though, and between the trees' interstices, it is impossible to not feel like he is walking into one. The edgeless expanse breeds dark shadows that limp and scatter like a stirred up flock of birds. He would like to find his way back home.

It may be a dream, so he finds a peeling piece of his cuticle and carves it out with his pocket knife. A thread, no more than a guitar string thick, curls from his body and he grabs it with one hand and pulls harder. His skin unwinds and he laughs. Blood pours, so it's not a dream, but his skin shears like tearing the scratch-cover off a mirror, so it is. He ties his flayed, threading skin around a tree branch and walks. A hundred paces later and he turns and his skin runs in a single, bloody line along the forest floor behind him. Already insects crawl from the dirt and taste him.

He walks farther. Each step takes a piece of him away. If it did not begin as a dream, he feels himself slipping into one now. Behind him, his skin; before him, the stranger's footsteps.

I think there's something wrong with us. The voice comes like a memory, but also from the trees. It sounds like Tyler's voice at first, but it's moldier. Tyler said that to him, once, before the end. They were ankle deep in cedar water. It was the summer and the sun was bright enough to taste. When they stepped out of the water their feet were pruney and they joked about looking old. *Do you think there's something wrong with us?* Trite wishes he had said no. Instead, he told the truth.

The forest floor has muddied, though there hasn't been rain in weeks. The footsteps are long gone and the sun is low enough in the sky for the trees to begin to poke holes in it. He knows where he is going. Behind him a long thin line of his skin leads back to the car. He thinks about severing the line, but only half of him has come undone. He is a vivisected drawing of a human in an anatomy textbook. He does not believe in half measures.

In the dream he is skinless and beautiful. The world is a smooth and textureless marble. There is nothing, absolutely nothing, to get hung up on, and Tyler is still alive. The half of him that's come undone is vibrant in the chilled air. The half of him remaining bucks against the branches and breeze. Half of him still feels everything, and everything is far, far too much for one person to hold.

He runs deeper. The trail of skin pulls taut and lifts into the air, sending the sphagnum and ants flying off it. He feels the tension of its reassuring pull as it unwinds down the inside of his leg. Stars dot the periphery of his vision and he runs faster. If it's not a dream, he wants to finish before he passes out. His leg is free and bleeding. The sticky muscle and tendon of his exposed body fills with dirt, sticks to branches and leaves, but he does not feel their intrusions because his skin is gone. There is pain, yes, but above the pain there is a singeing freedom that drowns it out.

His skin is almost all gone when he finds the tree. His tree, dead, still, but alive again, standing in the middle of the woods. All that's left is the skin of his face. The rest of him is free.

Once, he had thought that the world existed and it did not care about him or anyone he loved or anyone he hated and that was fine. He was different, but that was fine, too. Tyler told him that beneath the ground, the trees whisper to each other. They use mushrooms like nerve endings and all day and all night they cajole each other and laugh. He told him that at all times the earth is talking, and god is it loud. He listened with Tyler, he pressed his ears to the earth and strained with all his might, but he could never hear the under-noise. He had his own affliction of sensitivity. Tyler was the only one he told. He told him that light is both a particle and a wave, so anytime you are not in total darkness you are being completely caressed. *What does it feel like?* No one asked that question anymore except his therapist. They were afraid of Trite's answers. *It feels awful*, he told Tyler. *It sounds awful, too.* Tyler said. They were together, for a brief moment.

Now that Tyler was gone, he had no access to the cacophony, and no one who understood his tactile suffering.

His tree beckons, its void. He hopes it is not a dream. He hopes it is all real and this, this is the end of his feeling. He cannot enter with any skin remaining so he takes his thread gently between his bone-exposed fingers and pulls. Though he's hated his skin, he cherishes his final moments with it. Or, perhaps he cherishes its leaving. A long and sweet goodbye. His vision is almost all gone now. The blood feeds the sandy loam of the pine barrens at his feet. His skin rips from him, his lips coming off last in two tender filets. The tangled network of his yarned skin stretches for nearly a mile or seven—who can say this close to dusk?—behind him.

The void answers his sacrifice and widens enough for him to slide his barely stitched together bones through. Inside the tree welcomes him, coats his flesh in a hardened, dead bark that can hold him together without feeling anything. His new skin is all callous. He presses himself to the edges inside the tree and shimmies up, toward the blinding hole of white light above him.

The dead branches open like a crown. His bloody, masqueless face peers out and the light falls nervelessly upon him. He cannot feel a thing. Not a single thing. The sun is setting, now, while the tree holds him. The whole sky is the color of blushing cheeks. The world is quiet and touchless. In the dream, he is skinless and beautiful and the world is a smooth marble. In the tree he is crowned and singular. In the woods he is bleeding and lightheaded. In the car he is driving back home, the moon like sandpaper across his goosebumped and mud-caked skin, Tyler is dead, and nothing will ever feel safe to touch. It will be a coarse and gristled life. In the dream, though, in the dream he doesn't feel anything at all except safe, held by one of the only things that never made him feel worn through. Even then, he suspects, it will not be enough.

Her Alberta

Malcolm Devlin

ON THE FIRST-FLOOR LANDING, there was a door intended to remain locked. Late on her first night in the house, Ursula dreamed it was open and full of blackish, reddish hair.

In the morning, she woke, rested but fitful, and stood close by the locked door; listening to what she concluded was the deep in-and-out of a distinct and steady breath from behind it. When her sister, Ella, visited later that afternoon, she told Ursula she could itemise a dozen or more rational explanations for the sound even though she could hear nothing herself.

"In all other aspects, it's a pleasant house."

They sat across the table in the bright white kitchen. Ursula had made tea, but Ella had brought wine.

"You still need a job, of course."

Since their mother had died, Ella had said the same each day without fail. *You need to find somewhere to live. You need to find work.* Their mother, their mother's illness, was no longer an excuse. But to Ursula, the house was an occupation of a sort. "Work" felt like a faithless pursuit when she'd barely had time to become familiar with its rooms, its shapes, its airs.

When she had stayed with Ella during the months following the sale of the family home, Ursula would walk into town each morning because she imagined her sister's house was pushing her out like a splinter of wood under the skin. She would take a different route in and out of town every day, and at the end of one such hidden footpath, crossing the modest graveyard of St Peter's On The Hill, she found the house, standing alone in a shady cul-de-sac.

The house felt tall and narrow to her, the roof pitched a little too steep. It was red-bricked and orderly; high leaded windows flanking an attractive blue door. Two old and knotted apple trees grew on either side, softening the straightness of the walls and there was a painterly symmetry to the whole that was only disquieting when her back was turned.

As she passed it that first morning, she found herself stopping, backtracking, wanting to see. On her daily walks over the following few days, she made sure to pass by so she could see it again and again. It was the absence of it that haunted her.

There was no way by which Ursula could have known it was the very same place advertising for a house-sitter in the classifieds some weeks later, but she did. Those same windows, that same door, those same trees, peered out at her from between the printed words on the page. She had seen it and it had seen her.

"Six months is a long time."

Six months *alone*, Ella meant, as though it was something her sister had never yearned for since Ursula had moved in. Ursula rinsed the tea pot. Left it upturned on the stone countertop. Touched the surface with her fingertip.

"Six months is no time at all."

When she sat down again, Ella passed the letter back across the table. Ursula's hands, still wet, left dark moons, spreading through the warp and the weft, diffuse light on a cloudy night.

A single page, neatly typed, not signed.

Be well. Be happy. Your Alberta.

"Rather forward. Did you meet this woman?"

Ursula thought she might have seen her, once or twice. In the days she would change her route to walk past the house, she sometimes saw a woman through the window. Tall and lithe, high cheekbones and red hair in a spine-straight plait that reached down to her waist. A Pre-Raphaelite phantom flickering past the window as

Ursula lingered, stocky and self-conscious outside. But the house had been empty when Ursula had come in. The key was the only contents of the envelope she'd received in the post, its label lettered with the same typewriter that composed the letter she'd found waiting for her in the house's kitchen.

Make yourself at home. Keep the place clean. Leave it as you found it. Please don't open the door on the first-floor landing.

"American." Ella had an intuition about such things. Her Alberta, her imagined Alberta, was a rich American and this was just one of her houses. The house, she said, didn't look fully lived in. There was no clutter, no wear or tear. Everything was pristine and modern; fresh from the pages of a lifestyle magazine.

It was a rich woman's doll's house.

"And you know what that makes you?"

Ella lasted as long as the wine. It was dark when she showed herself out. A taxi was waiting for her even though Ursula didn't remember her calling one. Ella's wave goodbye was a brisk palm-print on the car's back window as it slipped away.

The quiet she left lingered, muting the next few days in an autumnal fashion. There wasn't much for Ursula to do other than to live; to occupy the space. She did her best, but the house made her see herself, and what she saw was gangly and off-centre.

She adopted a favourite chair in the lounge, one she could sit in and leave little impression. She began to read the books she found in the room she considered the house's library. Much of what she read, she wasn't certain she understood. They were books she hadn't heard of before. Serious works in sober jackets.

Ella had cautioned her she would need a job in order to feed herself, but the refrigerator and the larder, both of which Alberta's letter had invited her to use as she wished, never seemed to empty. There was always fresh milk, eggs and bread no matter how much she used. There were always dried goods, canned goods; there was wine, there were spirits, even though Ursula didn't drink.

The first letter came on her fourth day.

She'd been asked to leave any post on the desk of the study on the first floor. In practice, very few letters arrived.

This particular letter wore a large lilac envelope; it was

addressed to Alberta in blue-black fountain pen. Ursula didn't recognise the stamps or the postmark, both were smudged and distorted and difficult to read. She only knew that they were both unfamiliar to her.

She had no business reading the letter, but the flap was unglued and before she had concocted an excuse for herself, it was open and unfolded in her hands.

It was a simple thing. The author's name was Brammel, and in a few brief pages, she—Ursula assumed Brammel was a she— detailed a handful of family anecdotes as though to a friend. Her mother had left the hospital and was feeling much better but watching too many soap operas on the television; her brother, Ole, was home from his studies for the winter; he'd fallen off his motorbike and now had a scar across his jaw he was proud of. Brammel herself had a new exhibition on the horizon, but she wasn't confident in her work. She wished Alberta her love and her very best wishes and signed off.

Ursula folded the letter and returned it to its envelope. She placed it on the desk next to the typewriter, but the world of it stayed with her like the long fingers of an early evening shadow. How strange to read the careless intimacy of one stranger to another. The stories the letter contained, had been written as though they were already familiar and mundane, but to Ursula, there was a glittering promise of newness to them she couldn't quite define.

Later that evening, she returned to the study and sat down at the desk. She opened the bottom drawer and found a ream of clean, fresh paper. She threaded a sheet into the typewriter and rested her hands upon the keys.

My dear Brammel,

Her reply—if that's what it was—was brief. A simple thing in response to a simple thing. It was a senseless charade to enact, but it was a pleasant, strange, senseless charade. She responded to each anecdote from the original and offered encouragement to Brammel regarding her exhibition. She knew no artists and had little experience of her own to share, but her Alberta was wise on the subject. She was kind, but curt. Her prose sturdy with a wit that surprised her. Her advice was unadorned and straight to the point. It was *good* advice, Ursula thought. She concluded the letter in the same manner that Alberta had ended the document she'd found on the kitchen table.

Be well. Be happy. Your Alberta.

That night, she set the letter on the dressing table in the room she had chosen, and in her dream she opened the door on the first-floor landing to find a glistening, crimson post box had grown from the floor inside. Its slot was puce in colour and damp to touch. It took the letter from her and swallowed it and when Ursula woke, her palms were sweating as though they'd been licked.

A few days later, a new letter arrived. The same lilac envelope, the same muddied stamps, the same open flap.

My dear Alberta,

Ursula's replies were fluent in a manner that invigorated her. This was a new side to her and she relished it. Whenever Ella stopped by, Ursula found herself broken. She was smaller in her sister's presence than she was alone, and her sentences were stunted and clumsy.

In her letters, Ursula's Alberta was articulate. She was funny and disarming; her advice was smart and sound.

Brammel's brother had sold his motorbike and bought a truck, he had taken up with the girl who worked at the post office and by all accounts they made a handsome couple; their mother was well and well occupied; she'd taken up life drawing at the local community centre and she visited Brammel's exhibition in a wheelchair. Her mother was critical in that way of hers, but the exhibition was a sterling success and Brammel included a photocopied clipping from the local newspaper to prove it.

The letters continued to come and Ursula replied to them all. Her replies became longer and longer, each embroidered with increasingly elaborate improvised anecdotes. She found herself inventing biographical details about herself. Her Alberta had a sister and a brother. She had a dog named Max and a cat named

Oscar. The weather was always pleasant and there was music wherever she went.

Ursula never sent the replies, not in any way that made sense, but Brammel received each of them and received them warmly. She treated Ursula's invention as fact. She said she had *met* her brother. She'd seen pictures of Max and Oscar. She was intensely moved by Ursula's descriptions of the music she heard.

Alberta. I miss you so much. Every letter of yours makes me wish we were closer.

Ursula had been in the house for two months when Helga first came to visit.

There was a rapping at the door and there was a woman on the doorstep. A short woman in a tall fur coat and a curious, crooked hat. She looked younger than her manner in the powdery plastic way of the wealthy. She glowered at Ursula, then growled at her.

"Alberta. My dear, you look sick as a dog."

Ursula stuttered a correction. The woman's head angled sharply in response and Ursula wasn't certain she'd been heard, let alone understood. The woman flapped her hands.

"Well let me in, let me in. I didn't come all the way to this ghastly place to stand on your damnable doorstep all afternoon."

Inside, the woman, shrugged off her coat, leaving it in a furry puddle on the hallway floor. She seemed to grow without it, taking charge of the house as she moved from room to room.

"Well, we're not eating here."

The kitchen was spotless but the woman's nose wrinkled as she opened the refrigerator door and inspected the shelves.

"We are going out. I am taking you out."

She inspected Ursula with a critical eye.

"We shall have to find you something to wear. Follow me."

Ursula had only been in the master bedroom once. When she'd first arrived, she'd visited each room in turn. Other than her assumption it was Alberta's bedroom, there was little to suggest it was more personal or important than any of the others in the house. There was something of a show-house about it; a stage set; a diorama. To Ursula, however, the room *was* Alberta's, and as she knew nothing about the house other than this single name, it was a sanctum to her; conceivably even a holy one. She wouldn't sleep here during her tenure in the house, she decided. She wouldn't even enter it if she had no cause.

The woman had no such concerns. She flung open the wardrobe doors and ran her hands along the clothing hung within as though they were the taut strings of a harp.

"Let me look at you. Stand up straight. Up! Up! There. Now. Let me see."

Ursula complied, while the woman held dresses and suits against her, one after another after another, slapping them against her collarbone. Ursula dug deep inside herself and found the hollow where her voice had hidden itself. She asked who the woman was.

"Helga! Helga! Helga! Now. This, this, *this!* Put this one on and come downstairs. Don't dally, I'm hungry. Hungry! Helga is hungry."

Ursula, alone in the master bedroom, Alberta's clothes collected at her feet. A dark dress penciled in classic lines hanging from her hand. She thought of the woman with the long red plait. There was no way Alberta's clothes would fit her. The fabric was like liquid, the implied expense of it made her feel unwashed and unworthy.

Later that evening she would tell Brammel about the encounter in her letter and the words would tumble out of her, brittle and waspish; an anecdote sharpened to draw blood. Although she had no reason to believe such a thing, she told Brammel that Helga was her aunt. Wealthy and strange and desperate for attention. She loved her, of course, because family demanded such sacrifice, but *good heavens*, she said, it was a relief to be alone once she had gone.

Brammel would later reply with a letter of her own.

I haven't seen that woman for years. A menace! My word! My darling, how sorry I feel for you for having to entertain and endure her!

Helga had a car and the car had a driver. She hauled Ursula into the back seat like a carpet bag and barked a command which put the car in motion before the door had closed.

The cafe they found themselves in was not somewhere Ursula had ever been aware of before. It was somewhere exclusive, somewhere grand, somewhere hidden from the view of the passing public. Helga ordered for them both and talked the whole time without pause for response, which it seemed she neither wanted nor needed.

Was she Alberta's aunt? Was she a friend? A sister, a lover? Helga gave no clue to any possibility.

Ursula was happy to remain silent. She smiled, of course. In all the right places, she hoped, but in truth, the older woman's talk bewildered her. If there was a thread to it, it eluded her. If there was a point, it never landed. The subjects flared and died like fireworks and all Ursula could remember of them was the noise and the light.

They ate, although Ursula was not hungry. Small dishes she couldn't identify, by turns too salty, too sweet. Helga dabbed her lips with a handkerchief then sat back in her chair and regarded Ursula with a cat-like attention.

"She would like you. Alberta."

Helga's eyes narrowed a little, sparkled. She glanced up, then gathered her bag and ushered Ursula to her feet.

She didn't lead her to the exit, but to another room in the cafe. More tables, more chairs, a handful of people dining together and alone. There was art on the walls. A clutter of frames arranged to fill the space. Helga edged between the empty tables to approach.

"Do you see?"

The pictures were drawings. Pen and ink, rough but lively. Faces tangled in spirals and scribbles. It took a precious moment to understand their subject, but when one came into focus, they all did as though each portrait turned to face her at once. They were each of Ursula. Ursula asleep. Ursula alone. Ursula living in Alberta's house. Eyes closed, dreaming, breathing, a smile playing ever-so delicate on her lips.

Closer, she saw that each image was signed in the same way in the lower right corner.

B.

Helga was already done, already heading for the door.

"Well this was marvellous. Marvellous. We must do it again."

Alone in the house again, Ursula stripped out of the black dress and treated herself to a long bath. As she lay there, recalibrating to being by herself, she heard again the low sound of breathing from the door on the first-floor landing.

She dried herself and found a dressing gown, then sat on the floor beside the locked door and listened to the in and out and in and out and in and out.

There was something lulling about the tone and the rhythm of it. It reminded her of the nights she would spend in the wing-back armchair, listening to her mother sleeping in the bed beneath the living-room window. In and out and in and out and in and out; the occasional, precarious catch and whistle of breath.

On the carpeted floor of the first-floor landing, Ursula let herself drift to sleep.

She woke with a start, too early in the morning. The landing was cold and the shadows of the house in the stillborn hours were strange to her. She couldn't find her room in the dark, there was a seamless wall where the door should have been and it occurred to her, in a half-awake sort of way, that all her belongings, her clothes, her purse, were lost somewhere inside.

She went to the master bedroom instead. It barely felt like a trespass now that Helga had broken the seal.

She picked her way across the floor to the bed and slipped beneath the covers. As she fell, precipitously back to sleep, she was plunged back out into cold, rude wakefulness by the sudden conviction there was someone in the bed with her. She flustered, panicked then stilled. Reassuring herself she was alone, she slept until the early afternoon and for the first time since she'd been in the house, she did not dream.

Days passed, weeks chased after them, months followed.

Ella knocked on the door one morning and stood back waiting in the way she'd grown accustomed to.

The woman who opened the door looked at Ella as though she recognised her. A cat slipped through her legs, then disappeared inside. The woman smiled politely. She was, Ella thought, a woman who knew how to stand, to be still, affectless or disaffected.

"My sister was here. She was house sitting."

Ella said her name and the woman smiled and asked her to wait. When she returned she was carrying a letter in her hand, a lilac envelope, Ella's name typed in neat letters over and over and over again.

Silver Wires and Sweet Water

Alexander James

THEIR FLIGHT from the camp had gone poorly. Clem bore only a few scratches, but Jan had punctured his sole on a caltrop. Little Obol didn't even make it over the fence. As Clem ran the boy had called after them, tangled and weeping among the coils of razor wire, words drowned out by the shouts of the guards. Obol was dead the minute he'd got snagged, and Clem knew that he would be dead too if he'd stayed to help him. And yet.

"What did he say?" Clem asked as they stumbled deeper into the woods. "Before."

Their frenzied passage began to slacken, for they were unshod and clad only in their thin woollen uniforms. The trackless earth was a stew of broken ice and mud, cast into jagged trenches and crests that they picked across by moonlight. Ahead of them lay miles of wilderness, and the night was growing more bitter by the minute.

In the distance a siren whooped for a heartbeat, rupturing the silence before clipping off just as suddenly. *Strange*, Clem thought. *How they'd let us go so easily?* He awaited the rasp of engines or the baying of hounds to follow, but there was nothing.

"Don't worry about it," Jan muttered, long after Clem had expected any response.

Jan told Clem not to worry about a lot of things. He had seen it all before, he claimed, and worse. When Clem looked into the older man's face, those keloid scars crawling across his lips that dared you to shift your gaze...well, he was inclined to believe him. Before he'd been moved into the camp, Jan had been serving a sentence at the district prison. A *misunderstanding*, he claimed. Nobody asked any further.

They trudged onward as the moon shifted behind a gauze of clouds, washing the woods in ink. It was hard to believe it could get colder, but somehow it did.

"Where are we going?" Clem asked, eventually. It was getting difficult to think straight as the adrenaline leached away, leaving room for the deadening chill. Jan didn't look back at him. He just kept tramping along, leaf litter sticking to his bloody sock.

"South. We'll find something. A barn."

So, Jan didn't know either. Perhaps they'd both assumed they'd end up like Little Obol, torn up on the fence, or that the few cursory bullets shot into the treeline after them would seek their hearts. Perhaps they were already dead and this was their just reward. Clem chuckled at the notion until Jan hissed at him to be quiet.

After another few miles the forest began to thin out, old growth supplanted by copses of spindly birches and frozen ponds. Ahead was a thick band of black, darker than the star-littered sky. It soon resolved into a hedgerow, blocking their path as far as they could see in either direction. Jan pursed his ruined lips and blew through his teeth. For a long moment he said nothing and Clem braced himself. Then he muttered, replying to no-one. "Fine. Fine."

They scurried beside the ice-crazed ditch in the shadow of the hedgerow, weaving around shimmering expanses of black rime. Clem's coat grew stiff with his frozen vapours. His teeth began to chatter and his jaw ached with the effort of clenching it shut. His ears rang and his eyes unfocused and the world split into alternating panes of blues and blacks, shapes without meaning projected onto the back of his skull. He was conscious only that he was still moving, still breathing, when Jan spoke again.

"Up ahead."

Thorns gave way to a tall gate wrapped in knots of rusted chain. Beyond it lay not a manicured hunting ground or a country estate but an orchard, overgrown. Wiry brush had taken root and swamped the once orderly lines of trees, sinking them in a mass of waist-high grass and groping vines curiously untouched by frost.

They clambered over the gate and flopped into the marshy, sucking soil on the other side. Jan held up a finger and set off through the undergrowth. Despite his injury he remained quiet, and quick. Within a few seconds he was a shadow between the trunks, and then he was gone. Clem stamped his feet and clawed his hands as he waited, trying to work some measure of sensation back into them. His thoughts remained heavy, unable to be grasped, coated with the same unctuous matter that lines the threshold of sleep. He saw himself standing before Little Obol, trying to pull down the boys contorted body from the wire, both of them covered in tiny white hairs of frost that waved and waggled. Clem yanked at a rigid arm, and again, until it came away, snow-melt pouring out of the stump in an unending torrent, cascading over the chain-link in great gelid waves. The boy smiled and opened his mouth, and the sound of a gunshot erupted from him—

The sharp crack jolted Clem back to his senses. He followed the trail of flattened grass to a yard and a whitewashed cottage, the front door hanging drunkenly off a single hinge.

∾

INSIDE JAN WAS CROUCHED before a stove. Bluish sparks leapt and died with each shuddering match-stroke.

"Stupid, stupid," he said.

The cottage was old, but solid. Whoever had lived there had cared for the place. The kitchen was boxed by low dark beams, crowded with chairs and a table of heavy tannic oak. A straw basket sat atop it, half-filled with withered vegetables. Everything was coated in a film of dust. In the other room lay a toppled wardrobe and a bed strewn with discarded garments. Clem wondered what would have happened if Jan had found someone sleeping there and tried to put the notion out of his mind as best he could. Nobody had lived here since the war broke out. Before that, even.

Once they'd gotten the stove lit they slumped before it in a stupor, moving only to open the latch and rile the clammy logs with the poker. Clem felt sensation gradually burrow back into his limbs, itching and burning all the way.

"Where do you reckon the owners went?" He asked, once he could feel his face again.

Jan looked up. He'd torn a strip from the bedsheet and was wrapping it around his foot. A thin wet band between his eyelids shone. There was a hint of mirth, like he knew something Clem didn't.

"Don't worry about that."

"Just curious, is all."

"It's not important. What they leave behind...that's what matters," Jan said. "It spells opportunity for folk like us."

Clem didn't reckon he was much like Jan. He was a coward, yes, a deserter, but the other man was something altogether different. Clem had never had a *misunderstanding*. He looked away to the shadows dancing at the end of the room. Jan was still watching him when he turned back, no longer smiling.

"You and me. We had a deal. I've held up my end."

"Yes. Of course."

"Don't forget, now."

~

SEEMINGLY SATISFIED, Jan leaned back and stuck his bandaged sole toward the flames.

"Guessing you aren't in a talking mood," he began, "so I'll tell you a story. This place reminds me of when I went to stay with Nana. After my mother died and my daddy grew tired of...anyway. She owned a farm, is the point."

Clem waited for him to continue.

"Really, it was a few stretches of muddy pasture, unfit for much of anything but a few raggedy fowl and those horses she kept. Her pride and joy. Even on the nights we went hungry, there were oats enough to feed them. Oh, how she loved those horses.

"Except there was one Nana didn't like, not a bit. Had its own field because it would bite the other mares. She told me to stay far away from it, not to even look at it when I walked by if I could help it."

"Why?" Clem said.

"She saw it lure other animals past the fence. Chickens, mostly. Once or twice a squirrel or rabbit. Stupid, trusting creatures. Before they knew what was happening it would...stamp on them. Not enough to kill them, not immediately. Just with enough force to break a leg or a spine. To make them panic. Sometimes it would fling them up high in the air, play with them a bit before the end."

Jan paused.

"That creature just about hated every other living thing. You could tell from its eyes. It was smart enough to realise what side of the fence it was on and would always be on. Smart enough to be enraged by it."

The fire guttered. The moon was gone, and it was getting very dark now. Clem couldn't see Jan's face, only where the dying embers caught the hint of cheek or brow.

"She told me not to think of it as a horse. It was more like a thing stuck with a horse's body for its brief time on earth. A fact for which we should all be thankful. Do you understand what I mean?"

"What happened to it?" Clem found himself asking.

Jan moved his shoulders a fraction.

"It drowned in the floods. We cut it open, we were so hungry, but it was bad inside. "

They sat in silence as the warmth bled out of the room.

For the rest of the night they shivered in bed, stacked up against each other like kindling. It was better than being outside, but only barely. Clem tried not to move, tried to let the cold seep into and over him like he was a pebble in a lake. Behind his eyelids he could see Little Obol's drawn face, streaked with tears. He tried again to untangle the words from the chaos that had swallowed them, screams and gunshots and hoofbeats. There were little teeth, then an O, a black hole of a mouth contorting wider, wider. He must have said *go*. But before that? Was it *don't go? Just go? Let me go?*

Once or twice, Jan talked in his sleep. *Bad*, he muttered into Clem's hair. *Gone bad.*

~

THE NEXT MORNING Jan was sick. He spasmed and twitched and vomited stringy, acrid water into a pile of stale petticoats. With palsied hands he went to unwrap his foot. The skin was tight around the wound, and darkened tendrils crept outward from the margins.

"I think we need to find you a doctor," Clem said. He wiped his eyes at the fetor.

Jan laughed.

"And what will I tell them? That we're brave boys returning from the front? Patch me up and send us on our way?"

Clem said nothing.

"I just need to wash it out, that's all," Jan mumbled, tapping his fingers on his knee. "They'll have a pump or something around here. Won't they?"

Breakfast was a few shrunken potatoes baked in the ashes of the stove. They made Clem's stomach hurt. Afterwards, they changed out of their filthy uniforms for the oversized smocks of the former owner and some pairs of ill-fitting boots. They looked decent enough, but without any documents it was still too risky to travel on the roads. To reach Clem's village they would have to cut across the patchwork of fields and woodlands that made up the canton. If luck was on their side, they would find other houses on the way. And if not, they would walk all night.

Clem tried to ignore the thought creeping at the edge of his mind, the one that had been quietly gestating from the moment Jan peeled back his soiled bandage. It whispered to him that the other man was weakening, and soon he would be weak enough that Clem could lose him in the frozen woods. He couldn't have entertained such notions before, but circumstances had changed. He only had himself to worry about now. And despite their agreement, Clem couldn't lead this man back to his home. No. There was no telling what could happen.

And what if Jan guessed what he was going to do, another voice hissed? What if he caught up later, seeking to *misunderstand* him? Would it matter what Clem said, or did, at that point?

Jan eyed him as he tied up his boots, his expression unreadable. He must know, Clem thought, a spike of fear in his chest. He must know.

"Water," was all he said.

THE MIDDAY SKY was the colour of beaten tin. A thick fog had drifted in and draped mutely over the orchard, rendering the ranks of trees that emerged from the gloom as the endless sullen soldiers of some forgotten army. The fecundity of the place perturbed Clem. Maybe they had entered a valley last night without realising it, for every limb and sprig was burdened with garlands of green buds. Jan stayed out in front as he hobbled over the mushy ground. He was still fast, but every time his wounded foot came down he hopped as if he'd stepped on a coal.

They'd gone an acre or so when they stumbled across the cistern, hidden amongst a gnarled knot of underbrush. A bolus of moss-covered brick rose from the soil, capped with a bolted hatch.

"Here," Jan said. He clambered atop, and, after a couple of attempts, heaved the hatch away with a squeal of metal.

"Looks clean," Jan murmured, wiping his brow. "Too damn dark though——"

He opened his mouth to speak further but stopped. For a moment, an expression Clem had never seen on the man shivered across his face and then it was gone.

"What?" Clem said.

"There's something in there," Jan replied. "Down deep." He gave a brittle laugh and rose. "These farmers always hide something before they go. Opportunity, I told you."

Clem stepped before the hole. A rusted ladder descended the few feet of open air into a glassy vault of black liquid. There was no way of telling how deep it went. The interior walls billowed out into shadow, and Clem could make out nothing in the water beyond a few submerged rungs.

They found a bucket and fashioned a rope of old sheets. Casting it down and heaving it back revealed only clear water, denatured of any mystery in the wan light. Jan took a long draught of it and gasped. He offered it to Clem, who took a swig and promptly spat it out. The stuff was sour, gritty. It faintly burned his mouth.

"I don't think this is good water," Clem said. He was parched, but the thought of even another sip made him want to retch.

"Tastes fine to me," Jan grumbled. He poured the rest of the bucket over his foot. Clem watched the discoloured rivulets drain from his skin into the earth.

"What did you see down there?"

Jan didn't reply for a long time. He kept staring in the hole, before he lowered in the bucket again with exaggerated care.

"I don't know," he said. "Jewellery, maybe. It was long. Glimmering."

~

IT GREW apparent by the afternoon that Jan had no intention of moving on. He just kept pulling more buckets up, dredging for his obscure prize.

"Shouldn't we get moving?" Clem asked. "They'll be looking for us."

Jan didn't look at him, but the scars around his mouth grew taut.

"Nobody is coming for us. Go and make yourself useful."

Clem began to walk up the other side of the orchard, looking for the gate they had climbed over the previous night. On the way he plucked a few small, hard apples, skins puckered with tiny holes. As he was about to bite into one something tiny and colourless peeked out of a hole and retracted in again.

"Ugh."

After another acre the heavens opened. What started with fat droplets turned to stinging hail, and Clem was soon forced to beat a shivering path back to the cottage. Jan had returned before him, judging from the wet footprints to the closed bedroom door. The storm waxed, hail pitting against the tiny windows with a fury Clem feared was inexhaustible. It didn't let up even as the day slipped into night. Clem got another fire going. The stove popped and groaned as it warmed, scattering fitful licks of orange across the floor.

"Jan?" he asked through the bedroom door. "I've made a fire."

From within Jan spluttered something. *Go?* Clem tried the handle to find it had been wedged shut. He collapsed back into his seat, and as he mulled over the situation he slipped into a fitful doze.

He awoke to find Jan sat next to him, watching the flames. The older man looked worse, much worse. The skin around his mouth had peeled like a bad sunburn, revealing tender new flesh between the scars.

"What?" Jan said. He was rubbing his jaw absentmindedly.

"I think we should go tomorrow," Clem said. "Maybe we can find you some penicillin."

"I'm feeling alright," Jan said, slowly. "Better than earlier."

"You sure? You don't look so good. Something going on with your—"

He stopped himself, but Jan wasn't listening anyway.

"We aren't going until I get what's in that well. There's something special down there. I'm sure."

"You're injured. And we haven't got any food."

"We'll be alright for a few days. We've got water. And soon, we'll be rich. We can roll into your village like kings. Do what we want."

Clem swallowed.

"What about it?" Jan said. He leaned in. "You aren't thinking of reneging on our agreement, are you? Leaving your poor crippled pal to fend for himself? That's your style, I know."

"No. That's not—"

"Good. Because you wouldn't last a minute out there, on your own. They'd catch you and do you worse than your Little Obol. You'd tell them I was here."

"I wouldn't. I swear."

"You would. I know you would, because I'd do the same."

Before Clem could protest further Jan raised his hand. In the half-light it looked puffy and poreless, a glove one size too big.

"All I asked for was a place to lie low," he said, softly. "Until this ugliness sorts itself out. You told me you knew a place. Quiet. Nice folks. Pretty girls. Remember?"

Clem nodded. Whatever it had taken to get him and Little Obol passage, he had said it, and more.

"Good. So no funny business, now."

That night Clem slept propped up in his chair. From behind the bedroom door he would sometimes catch the fragment of a sentence, the fallen fruits of some violent and clotted dream. Clem looked down at the poker by the stove, back to the door. Back to the poker.

~

THE NEXT MORNING Clem was roused by a searing ache in the small of his back. A tendril of dried blood came away when he rubbed at the corner of his cracked mouth. Jan was gone. He'd left behind bedsheets crumpled up, stiff and streaked with dark stains.

Overnight the orchard had flooded into a miniature sea, a mirror tarnished with spiny islets. Clem cupped a hand, reached down and took in some turbid water. It tasted sour, still, but less so, and he just about forced it down. Jan pacing before the cistern, stripped to the waist, whistling as he swung his arms back and forth, kicking up great sprays from the miry earth. The limp was gone, as was the queer rash his face had incurred the day before. Something else had changed in him too, although Clem couldn't tell exactly what, at first.

"I feel good," Jan said. He stretched and popped his joints. "Must be the country air."

Clem stole another look in the hole. Maybe Jan was right. There was something in the water, or the suggestion of something, an interruption where the travel of your eye snagged like a barb. At first he had mistaken it for the play of light on the surface. It was something either very small or very far away, something twisting and diaphanous hanging in the void. Silver wires.

Jan tied the cloth rope around his waist and the other to the topmost rung of the ladder. He threw the rest into a heap atop the bricks.

"If I'm down there too long you pull me up, understand?"

How long was too long? Clem was about to ask. Then he noticed the scars on Jan's mouth had shrunk to white threads, nearly invisible, and he suddenly felt very afraid. He managed to nod.

"Alright, then. When I get tired, it's your turn."

Jan clambered inside and dived off into the blackness with barely a splash. Clem watched him swim down, down. The rope unspooled and wound behind him like an umbilical. Soon he was a pale shape, a speck, and then he was gone.

When he was sure the other man was deep enough, Clem kicked the rest of the rope into the water. A shower of black needles flew across his vision, yet he managed to keep enough grip to force the hatch back into place and yank the bolt across. Afterwards, he panted and retched, and rose on unsteady feet.

It took Clem a long time, for the gate was not where he had remembered it, and he was feeling rather weak now, his stomach trying to digest itself, thick bile coating his throat. But then all of a sudden there it was, the spindly ironwork listing drunkenly in the quagmire. He took a step toward it, and then another, up to his shins, then knees. The water prickled and nipped at his skin. He waded through until he could reach the bars and hoisted himself up.

From his vantage point it was clear the woods were now a swamp, had always been a swamp, a fact elided in their initial flight by the shadows and frost. It was no wonder they hadn't been pursued. Despite his mounting panic, Clem knew it would be suicidal to venture out now between the long dark pools and the birches. The day was nearly through. One false step and he could drown, or be left for the chill to finish the job. The sky turned the colour of a bruise while he swayed atop the gate. *Go*, the small pale voice pleaded, insistence bordering on hysteria. *You can't stop. You can't stay. Go, now. He's still here, in the water.*

But there were still a few logs left by the stove, enough to comfort him for one more night.

On his way back through the glittering undergrowth Clem passed the hatch again. He got on his hands and knees and put his ear to it. On the other side of the metal there was silence. Clem awaited the guilt, the guilt he understood would gnaw at his insides and eat him up like people said it did when you did wicked things, but he only felt tired.

The cottage was exactly as he'd left it. Once he'd gotten a feeble flame going, Clem sank back into his seat. Just a few hours. Enough to warm him up. He would depart before first light.

∾

WHEN CLEM AWOKE NEXT, he didn't understand for a few moments what he was seeing. Then the dread squirmed up within his chest. He should have left already. He should have left when he had the chance. Jan was standing at the other end of table, faceless in the grainy predawn light. The other man was naked, shining and distended as a blister. Clem slowly reached for the poker by his feet. He couldn't tell if Jan's head was turned towards him or not. His whole body was rippling.

"Thank God," Clem managed to force out. "The hatch got stuck. I couldn't open it. I was going to get help—"

"Don't worry about it," Jan replied, thickly. His voice sounded like it was coming from inside Clem's skull. "I would have done the same."

Neither of them spoke. Clem wrapped his fingers around the poker.

"I'm going to go, now."

Jan muttered something in reply, too quickly and quietly for Clem to catch. He stopped and coughed, wetly.

"They were far down. Too deep. Had to drop the rope. But I found lots of them. They always hide something."

Something translucent twisted at the edge of Jan's silhouette, retracted.

"They just need a place to lie low. Like us."

If Clem was quick he could get past the other man to the door. He rose, preparing to bolt, but found himself off-balance, the floor now a skin stretched over some dense liquid. His ankle rolled and he toppled awkwardly, stabbing the poker down, then through. The next few seconds were a blur. Clem clawed madly as the floor flapped and sank and everything went with it into the darkness. Behind him the stove crashed and hissed. Something heavy struck his head and chest, shoving him under. Without thinking he opened his mouth to gasp, and the water rushed in.

PALE SUNLIGHT STUNG Clem's eyes. Sodden clothes stuck to him and he knew he should have been freezing, but a strange and not unwelcome warmth instead suffused his body. It was about time he left. He felt strong, stronger than he had felt for a very long time, but his legs didn't want to obey him. He just about managed to get up, to stagger across the solid floor.

The fog had burnt off to reveal blue skies. Out in the orchard he could see his skin was looking real bad, but it didn't hurt. It only tingled a little, fizzing with something he didn't yet know was a promise. Now that he was free, he would go back. Back through the woods, back to the fence where they'd left Little Obol hanging, crying. Clem could take him down. He could listen to what the boy had wanted to say. And after that, he could rest for a moment. Just a moment.

He followed a gentle downhill slope that he wasn't sure had

been there before, leaning against the trees whenever he got too dizzy, until he reached the cistern. The hatch was open and the water inside had risen to the lip. On closer inspection, it was over-flowing, the meniscus breaking out and over the sodden bricks in a steady pulse.

Clem was very thirsty. More than thirsty. He wanted to dive in, to feel the water against his skin as he submerged himself, deeper and deeper. He bent and looked down into the hole. For how long he wasn't sure. A knot of torn cloth flapped around the ladder's top rung.

"Jan?" Clem called into the water. He felt suddenly foolish for doing such a thing, but then he saw there was something down there after all. It had been tiny and far away but now it was getting bigger, closer, still indistinct but not for much longer. It wasn't Jan. Clem stared and stared as it rose up, and when he finally figured out the coiled outlines of it, what it meant for him, he tried to step away but he found that he couldn't. Instead, the earth moved, just a little, a sheet tugging under his feet. All the trees around him stuck out at wrong angles and the parts of his brain that could still register fear began to whimper.

Then the floods rose over the tops of his boots, and that was all the understanding the things inside of him required.

Nothing Good Without a Price

Martin Cahill

AROUND THE END of each year, you stop asking questions. You all do. And you've been here long enough that what was once horrifying has since become boring. Commonplace. A fact of the universe.

Birds fly to warmer climates, running from the cold. Wasps freeze, leg by leg, gold and black statues inside their quieting hives. Mammals seek the bowels of mountains, entombing themselves in crypts of stone until totally exhausted, their empty stomachs bringing them back to weak winter light.

You and your coworkers at the call center stop asking questions.

Though, to be fair, asking questions never seems to produce answers. Just friction. Tension that could be felt in every cubicle, every little huddle of coworker waiting for the elevator.

Eventually, you heard that Wendall, a big question guy, received an email from his own email address. It said, *Questions cost.*

It was around the third tooth falling out of his mouth that he stopped asking questions. Some have heard he keeps them in a little box on his desk. When you hear the faint rattle of bone hitting metal, you know he's shaking that box, meditative; you know he's weighing the chance at knowledge against tooth number four.

But that's not your business, nor anyone else's.

Especially when there's work to do. Calls to take. Emails to flag. Lies to speak.

DIXIT '25

It varies, but it's usually around when the clocks change. When night stretches, and blooms. When light shrivels. That's when those first calls start rolling in.

Just a trickle, a handful here and there. But they're enough to convince Vince and Andy to get the corkboard from the storage closet; they use it to track bets. Small ones, they say each year. Inconsequential, really. Stuff like who gets the most calls, who can stay on the line the longest, who will be the first to vomit; lightweight stuff. That's all.

Again, just because questions can't be asked doesn't mean answers can't be . . . cobbled together. You've been here long enough to figure it out . . . most of it. Kind of. Even thinking you know exactly what sends your heart racing. Not for the reason someone new might think. Not because it's amoral. Or bone-chilling.

It's because if you really let yourself figure it out, you don't think you could fake ignorance. That all it would take is one slip-up, and the powers-that-be might let you go.

And losing this job? It would kill you.

Deirdre was close. Like you, she'd stopped asking questions. But she hadn't stopped trying to assemble the puzzle, to see the big picture. Over company holiday drinks, voice low, Santa hat askew, she'd whispered to you that she was close. She'd said, "It's the way some of their voices change on the phone. When you call them back? It's . . . you know what I mean! They don't sound the way they did before, when they were starting to scream—"

Bob in HR had suddenly appeared, cheeks red, reeking of rum, spewing uncomfortable jokes about a tradition called a White Elephant.

You never told Deirdre that you saw him turn on his heels and head right for you, like he could hear her over the din.

Again, not like it's your fault. You don't want to put it together. She chose to do it, to bring those disparate pieces together, and when the email was sent in January saying Deirdre was quote-unquote off to greener pastures, you did what you learned how to do here: you didn't ask questions.

There are some things worth compromising on, if it means you can survive.

But even after almost a decade with Mooneye Security Systems Inc., it's still hard to receive those first few calls. It takes until after Thanksgiving to build up the thick skin needed in order to weather the rest of the calls you know are coming through the new year.

At least the first few are . . . well, not easier than the later ones. They all suck. Even poor Gerard, here twenty-nine years and counting, admitted in the company All-Hands last Spring that he hates the end of the year.

But in his own words, sandpaper rough through chain-smoker phlegm, "We're the best damn security in the United States, and always fucking have been. There's a reason for that. There is! Because the strongest security isn't free, and nothing good comes without a price. Only death is free, fuckers!"

And then Helen in HR, Bob's replacement, clapped her hands and said it was time for snack break, and ushered Gerard to the side for a surprise call from Corporate.

Whatever they'd said to him must've been good, because when he came back his smile was huge, even as blood wept down from the corner of his eye, like a teardrop.

Corporate can't be everywhere though, and no matter how they try to smooth it over, Gerard's right. End of the year sucks, and those first few calls, hard as they can be, are just the warmup.

You still remember your first one, the autumn you were hired; everyone remembers their first. You still hadn't really understood the instructions emailed that said, *End Of Year Call Script October 31ˢᵗ – January 1ˢᵗ*.

But you did your best to follow them, even when it felt weird. Even when it told you not to offer certain solutions, or suggested reasons to hang up on them. Even when you came across language you didn't recognize, which left search engines scratching their head. You tried to Google a symbol, and your laptop made a sound like a cat screaming, and the keyboard letters that make up your name shattered, one after the other. To this day, going to Google redirects you to a website called, "PermissionNotForgiveness.com," regardless of the computer.

After a while, it became rote.

Just like everything else.

The end of October brings the early calls. Those vaguely panicking folks, working to keep the fear out of their voice as they tell you that for some reason, their Mooneye Security Home Satellite system isn't disarming so they can leave their home. Yes, they tried that code. Yes, they tried to reset it. Yes, they'd hold, but also, my husband has to get to work, could you—

Hold for three minutes. One hundred and eighty seconds is a lifetime for the worried.

Off of hold, there's the nervous laughter, the rueful tone. Wow, I'm silly, they'll say. I guess it was just some kind of update.

Of course, you intone, warmth with no heat, fire with no light. Those can happen. Especially towards the end of the year.

And when they ask why, you go, I wish I knew, but I'm just in Customer Service. You'd have to talk to Engineering. But I'm glad I could help you today.

Of those calls and the one's that appear right around Daylight Savings at the start of November, you know perhaps half of them will be marked with a small green check-mark on your Teams folder. You used to think it was some wonky algorithm, claiming certain houses for follow up. And in a way, you're right.

Now you know better: those customers of the green check-marked houses? They're the ones who didn't ask a lot of questions.

It makes what comes next easier. For the folks upstairs at least. Not for you, and certainly not for the people.

But it's like Gerard said, and the man in shadow on the Corporate Zoom meeting, and that voice in your first moments of waking that sound like your dead Mother and the hasty abortion you got in college: nothing good comes without a price.

Most of November are emails complaining that the Customer Service number isn't working or sending people right to voicemail; you know that happens to give the system a break before the December rush.

And so, people send emails.

I woke up at 3am and my bedroom window was open, wide open! My system was plugged in but it was dark? Fresh batteries after I called a few weeks ago, just to be careful, but now it isn't working, and my window was unlatched? Lock is on the inside of the house, obvs, but this is weird. Please call me back.

Dog almost dead. Car started in garage. Garage filled with exhaust. No alarm, nothing, squat. Fucking almost killed Cookie, she is small chihuahua, size of big rat, small lungs. Who the fuck put her in the car? No keys in ignition. Mooneye stayed green, said all is fine. All is NOT FINE. CALL ME BACK.

Hi there! Thank you for your help in advanced. I am the owner of the Mooneye Lunar Watch Cam system, as we have decent acreage, and the extra eyes help, ha! Last night, we heard noise in the front yard, and a loud banging came from our front door. Cameras saw no one, and did not report an intruder, which is concerning, but we thought it was the wind, maybe. This morning, it took an hour for the system to turn off. When we went outside, two muddy footprints were on our front stoop. Looked like someone walked through a swamp, with no shoes on? Footprints went to the backyard and stopped suddenly. Any help would be great! Thank you. Oh, my husband wants to know how to turn off that buzzing sound?? I don't know what he's talking about, but I told him I would ask. Thanks! Have a great day! =]

In the key of Cambria and Times New Roman, to the tune of Helvetica, Aptos, and Garamond, even some discordant fucking Comic Sans, you all read through the customer emails each morning that first week of December.

Word comes down from Corporate on December 8th. It's time.

That's when you all, collectively, turn your brain off. Consciousness go bye-bye. Morality, too. The only compass by which to steer is external, now.

It's the only way to survive what's to come.

At midnight, December 9th, phones ring incessantly. There are so many of you working, here, overseas, overtime, that no phone goes unanswered. Everyone picks up. Everyone says, "Mooneye Customer Service, how can we help you?"

Everyone hears something different.

On her truncated lunch break, Helga, her third year here, wipes blood from her nostrils as she recounts that the first six calls she picked up had no voices, just something that sounded like a chainsaw, retorting endlessly until the mandated three-minute wait passed and she was allowed to hang up. You hear her vomiting later in the bathroom. At least she didn't cry, (that was a year one and two usual).

Quinn is seen leaving their cubicle, face blank, dark face ashen, and they take their glasses off, a wedding ring off, and start taking off their tie, undressing as they leave in no real rush. But you know Corporate flagged Quinn; it's their first year. Luckily, you hear later, someone stopped them from walking into oncoming traffic. Only clipped by a sedan, and that, only going twenty miles an hour. They'd be back tomorrow. You know they can't afford to lose this job.

When you see them the next day, icing their hip, tongue touching the tender spot where a tooth had been knocked loose, your baleful gaze must have held the question, one you know you couldn't ask aloud, and they still said in a voice rich with shame, "It's . . . I couldn't stop hearing it. The baby. The baby in the background. Crying. Even when it stopped, I—"

You left them so they could sob in peace. But you breathed a sigh of relief when their phone rang, and automatically, they responded, voice steady and even. Good. They'd get through it.

You all would, barring a few truly rough calls. For the most part, yours fit the standard of what you've come to expect.

Yes, we are seeing some unusual activity in your neighborhood. Please stay in your home. Help is arriving shortly. The lights? Yes, it makes sense they're out. We're seeing—yes, a technical difficulty. You're so right, I hate when that happens. Remember, please stay inside, we're seeing a network issue that could be affecting streetlamps, who knows what's going on out there. Music? Maybe, I can't hear anything on my end, but—yes, certainly possible. People play music at all sorts of odd times. Childhood lullaby? Isn't that interesting? Hang tight. Please hold.

Yes, we are seeing that your Mooneye has lost power. Not sure why that's affecting your door locks and keys, those should be working. Are you members of Mooneye's Constellation Program? Our Stars in the Program have shorter wait times for local engineers to come and inspect —Oh, I'm so glad you asked. Right now, we have a holiday sale that comes out to about sixty dollars a month. Fifty, if you refer a friend to our system and Program within six months of—yes, there's a rebate. Oh, hmm, I'm not sure why the temperature in your house is dropping. You can see your breath? And it says here, you're in Arizona? Well, that's bizarre. Please hold.

Yes, we are seeing that there's been a surge in your county. Affecting many electronics, of course, and—well, I am aware you have a back-up generator Mr. Stern, but have you given it a thorough inspection? When was the last time? Hmm, while that falls out of the normal window, I have someone coming on through who could look at it while they inspect your Mooneye Security System. Oh . . . Hmmm . . . well, were they at home asleep when this happened? Oh, Mr. Stern, I don't know where your kids would be at 3am if they weren't asleep, but I'm sure they just got scared and hid. You know kids. No, I don't have any of my own, but we were talking about—ah! There we are. There's an engineer coming your way. He's going to text you when he arrives, he'll need your permission to enter. Oh, it's all very standard, Mr. Stern. I could pull up the whole consensual dialogue but—yeah, yeah. That's his number. Just go ahead and write back yes. He's going to take care of you all in no time, just as soon as you approve his request. Maybe even help you find those kids! Okay, I'll wait to hear back. Please hold.

One by one, the calls end. There are a lot of reasons, and you all compare at the Keurig machine.

The line eventually went dead, the dial tone flatlining.

Power going out in the house entirely.

And sometimes, a different voice altogether speaking, and in a terrible monotone, they say, "Thank you. We are satisfied."

No one can agree on what that person sounds like; some think they all sound the same. Others think they do not.

No one asks any questions.

The New Year arrives. Mooneye stock is up, yet again. And that bonus comes in, independent of the holiday bonus and the extra vacation time, and the Mondays in January off, because everyone just did so well in this time of crunch and sacrifice.

Bonus means groceries. Doctors. Braces. Repairs. Clothing. Diapers. Diplomas. School. Bills. Taxes. Technology. Vacation. Fuel. Nights out. Theater. Indulgences. Experiences.

It means providing, for yourself. For others.

It means sweet, sweet life gets lived, and your life remains uncomplicated.

You can't think about those on the phone. Those other lives. Those families. Like any good employee of Mooneye, one that lasts, one that goes places, you've stopped asking questions.

At this point, you can't think of any answer that would make anything better anyway.

All calls die down until about March. Then, new families move in. With neighbors that don't know where those previous home-owners went. But hey, welcome!

It's strange, one mother says to you, thrilled at having her dream home and yet confused, but we couldn't turn down such a good opportunity. Not with the school district we're in now. And didn't we get lucky, having a brand-new Mooneye Security system installed only a few years ago! Isn't that crazy? Aren't these super expensive?

Oh, yes ma'am, you say, they certainly can run a pretty penny. But you know what they say. Nothing good comes without a price. And lucky for you, the previous family paid for you!

You both laugh. If she doesn't hear the hollowness in your voice, that's not her fault. You think that's just kind of how you sound now.

You look up. Your floor manager, Theresa, heard what you said. She nods once, gives you a thumbs up, and makes a mark on her clipboard.

You clear your throat and try not to feel so proud.

In this job, you've got security.

And as you know, the strongest security isn't free.

As you sign up this ecstatic new homeowner, watching her through her new Mooneye lens, you start to cry, even as you laugh with her about how yes, it is funny, customers are called Stars in the Constellation Program. So clever, the folks in marketing.

Behind her, you see it. There is a too-tall man, pale, standing in her kitchen. No shadow. He is naked. In his right hand, a pristine cleaver. His lower jaw is missing, but in his eyes, you see curiosity. Appraisal. Appetite sated for the moment, and yet.

He looks in the lens. Blinks, like he sees you, too.

Vanishes.

At the end of some year, maybe soon, he'll be hungry again. Him and who else. What else. And in the meantime, a lot like you, he'll be watching.

For the first time in many years, you can feel your gut knot up, like you might vomit.

Nothing good comes without a price.

And you know, no matter what comes next, you'll be paying for a long, long time.

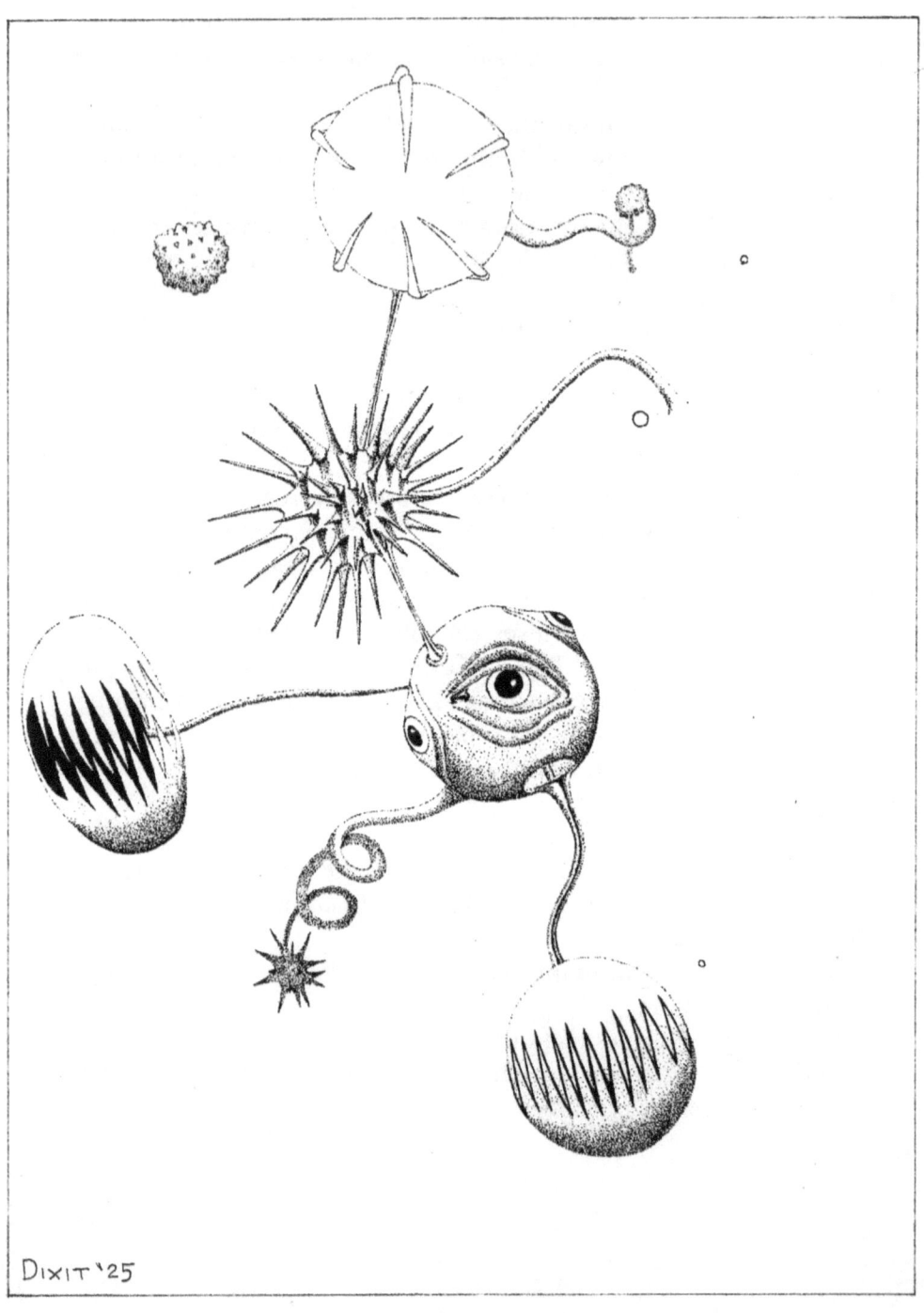

DIXIT '25

Scratch Dinner

Françoise Harvey

"WELL, WHAT A KIND THOUGHT." Mam holds the plant in front of her as though she'd quite like me to take it back. She did the same thing with the birthday card, frowning at the words I worked so hard to write. My fingers are inclined to let the ink smear and the pen wobble. The plant, which had dark green, spiked, upright leaves when I bought it, has also smeared and gone wobbly. It's dropping brown-blotched leaves on the kitchen table. There's a chip in the pot that I didn't notice before. "There was no need."

"I wanted to," I say. Mostly true.

"I'll find somewhere for it." She puts it down, turns to the fridge. "Dinner, then? Just a scratch meal." I catch the sideways slide of her look. "Beetroot, lettuce. Boiled egg? Tomatoes. Nice and filling." She starts chopping the tomatoes into wedges.

"I'll butter some bread, shall I?" I offer.

"No need," she says. Tomatoes done, she discreetly moves the knife well over to the other side of her, out of my reach. It's a good one, that knife. Old, and Dad kept it sharpened to a sliver. He used to use it to joint rabbits for stews.

The thought of a proper meaty stew makes me hungrier. I pull a slice of bread out of the packet and eat it unbuttered, collecting the crumbs with my thumb so I don't waste any. It doesn't help.

Mam twirls the half-et pack neatly closed and drops it in the bread bin. Another leaf falls off the sad spiky birthday plant. I feel sorry for it. When I bought it, I'd some notion I was rescuing it from the bitshop. The gardening section there was just a steel cage with wheels, its shelves crammed with too much greenery. The way the leaves shivered whenever anyone walked past put me in mind of fish and hamsters in large pet shops, huddling away from the overhead lights and the vibrations of curious fingers tapping on the glass. I know how that feels.

"Ellie's coming over in a bit," I say, to fill the disappointing silence. "She's bringing a cake." My guts twist, immediately. It hits like that sometimes, my stomach knowing I've done something wrong before my brain does. "Oh."

Mam frowns. "What?"

"I think the cake was supposed to be a surprise," I say. Another fact surfaces that I think she might like: "Ellie helped me pick out the plant."

Mam brightens. "One of hers, is it?"

I dodge that question. Ellie runs some sort of online influencer shop selling plants and other things that people who like plants like. I'd hinted to her about Mam's birthday, hoping she might give me something nice for free that I could give as a present, but she said she could only offer mates' rates. Her other mates must be million-aires. When I'd started whinging, though, about buying Mam an *unethical gift* grown *who knows where,* Ellie cut me off. "You're wearing a t-shirt from Primark, Tannie," she said. Then she got distracted by a display of ugly little plastic turtles with air plants glued to their backs.

I should have been annoyed, but it was pleasing, that comment and her distraction. We were friends again for a moment—not babysitter and babysat.

"She thought you'd like it," I tell Mam. "And you barely need to do anything to look after it, she said."

"Oh well, that's good of her," Mam mumbles. "Though I've never had green fingers. Not nurturing enough, I suppose." She puts a nearly empty plate in front of me, and takes a bite of beet-root herself. I stare at her teeth, bloody tombstones, and watch the way the lines around her mouth move marionette-like when she chews, and I almost feel at home. Then she smiles her formal smile, and the feeling's back. The one of being shown around your own old house like a stranger, by someone grown strange.

"I'll be out of your way soon, Mam," I say, trying to lessen the tension. "I'll sort things out with Marty."

Mam coughs, beetroot catching in her throat.

"There's no rush," she says. "The spare room's spare for a reason." The spare room used to be my room, but my room was split in two. Now half of it's a locked cupboard filled with all the junk no one wants. The other half is a bed and a bedside table with a bible in the drawer.

Doorbell, thank goodness, and then Ellie lets herself in shouting, "Hello, only me!" She has a covered plate in her hand, make up on, hair fresh done. She's *Made An Effort*. She's brought proper presents.

Mam smiles properly for Ellie, and they hug—cosy and swaying. Then Ellie hugs me, too, but in the careful way she uses with me, not too close. Still, at least she does it. I sniff her skin—too perfumed—and admire the jumping pulse in her neck. I turn back to my lunch. My stomach rumbles. The lettuce doesn't look organic. I prefer organic.

Mam opens Ellie's presents eagerly, and displays a pendant necklace and a matching pair of earrings. The pendant is a little glass globe, like a marble, with colours twisted inside. The earrings are glass, too, and tear-shaped, with a similar pattern of reaching colours. She dangles them in my face.

"Look, Tannis! Ellie, did you make these?"

"Yes!" said Ellie. "New line for the shop. I got the idea while we were shopping, Tannie. I made some for me, too." She is wearing them—a necklace and earrings. The same design.

I have to blink a few times to see it properly, but I realise: Ellie's basically given Mam greenery for her birthday, too. But she's given her three plants, and they are *creative*. They are the jewellery—the patterns in the little glass danglies are tiny, tiny air plants, in greens and blues and reds, leaves reaching out to press the sides of their enclosure. They look sharp and spiteful. I like them about equal to how much I hate Ellie just then.

"Like a ship in a bottle," Ellie's explaining. "There's a little hole in the pendant, and I put the plants in and then they settle down and spread out."

"Won't they die in there?" I say. Mam shoots me a slap-look.

"No," says Ellie, too pleased with her creation to notice or care that I'm narky. "Air plants don't need soil. Wear the jewellery out in rain, or hang them in the bathroom, for the humidity, and they should be fine. They like to be neglected."

"Nothing *likes* being neglected," I say.

"Not everything requires the amount of attention you do, Tannis," says Mam. "I'm going to put my beautiful new jewellery on right now. Thank you, Ellie." She hurries out of the room, already unfastening the wooden beads she usually wears. She'll put them away. Everything must be in its place, immediately.

Once she's gone, Ellie turns to me.

"Tannis, I've got something for you, too. For your room."

"I'm moving out soon," I say, but I reach for the gift box anyway. My hand shakes as I do, and Ellie and I both stare at my trembling fingers for a second, the nails cut to the quick. I force my hand to grab the box and put it in my lap.

Ellie purses her lip. "Tannie, did you know Marty woke up?"

"I—" I don't look up straight away. I can feel Ellie leaning towards me, like she's eager for something. But I don't know if Mam told me. Did she? Would she tell Ellie and not me? Maybe she did tell me and I forgot. "Maybe."

"He's been saying all kinds of things, Tannis. I just wanted to warn you…" She touches my sleeve, then freezes, head tilted listening for Mam's return. Her fingernails are polished all perfect. I can smell them. "Anyway, you need to let go of the idea that you'll be moving out. You have to stay here, remember? The judge said, and the doctors."

"What judge?" I remember the doctors.

"*Ellie*," Mam snaps from the doorway.

Ellie stands. "I'm just trying to make sure she understands."

"She understands enough."

"I don't," I say. "You don't tell me anything. You don't even feed me properly."

Ellie looks at my near-empty plate and then at Mam and shakes her head.

"There's nothing wrong with a scratch dinner," says Mam, defensively. "I've not got much in at the moment. And besides—"

"Besides *what?*" interrupts Ellie, but she says it quite gently. "Bolognese, stew, meat, three veg, the usual. The doctors said she needs to eat properly…"

"That's not what *she* means by properly, though, is it?" says Mam. She hisses *she* with so much venom that I almost don't realise *she* is *me*. Mam runs out of the room. Ellie follows her. After a few minutes, I pick up Dad's jointing knife from the sideboard, and I take it and my present upstairs and wait.

Ellie leaves shortly after. I hear the door shut. And Mam can't have been too mad at her, because when she comes upstairs with supper she still has her new jewellery on, and she even gives me another slice of bread, with butter this time. I push it aside, ask for a slice of ham, or maybe a bit of stewing steak. But she looks at me with that flat, blank, stranger expression and locks my bedroom door without answering me.

So I open my not-birthday present from Ellie.

Nestled in shredded cardboard are three glass spheres, each a different size. They're attached to each other by fishing wire, so when you hold up the hook from which they hang, they drop in a line, from largest to smallest. The largest is about the size of a grapefruit, the smallest a golf ball. They're very light, the spheres; the glass is thin and delicate. They chime a little as I untangle them. Each globe has a largeish hole cutout near the top. Inside them, more air plants. I've never seen them like this, all these colours. I'm only used to the shrivelled grey-green husks like in the bitshop. But these are purples, blues, reds, all with a silver sheen, and their skinny leaves reach to skim the curve of their enclosure, straining up and round, like lightning in a plasma ball, but frozen.

There's a leaflet in amongst the shredded cardboard. *Air plants live off the air and water in the air. The presence of plants in a home can help reduce anxiety and aid mental health. Air plants require very little care, but offer a lot in return! These plants are organically and sustainably grown and were sourced from…*

The print here is smudged and I can't make out the rest.

I like that they're organic. I tap the biggest sphere gently, and the leaves inside shiver and shimmy. I can see the plants' wiry little non-roots pressed against the bottom of the spheres, and it seems obscene to be able to see this private part of them, like studying someone's pubic hair. I decide to name my plants. The largest is Biggun. Below is Betty. Betty is in Biggun's shadow. The smallest is Baby. Baby already looks somewhat shrivelled and abandoned. It doesn't look as though it likes being neglected.

There is another, tiny note in Ellie's spidery writing. She *loves* me, she has written, *no matter what*. She knows I'm *not a bad person*. I *must remember that*.

The note warms me. If Ellie will love me anyway, then I can carry out my plan without guilt.

I take the jointing knife, sharpened to a sliver, and I cut a careful line on my bicep. It doesn't hurt. I flex a few times, the better to get the blood flowing, and then I lick. I lick and lick, tenderly, my arm. It reminds me of being younger, practicing kissing on my hand, and I close my eyes and imagine I am licking Marty: the iron taste, the musk, the salt. The cut stops bleeding too soon, and I make three more before my stomach stops rumbling. My arm stings a little, and my lips feel dry and sore from licking, and I'm quite thirsty. I almost call Mam for water, but I'm angry with her right now, though I can't quite recall why. The reason dissipated somewhere in the midst of the hunger pangs. Something about Marty. She never talks about Marty, even though I want to.

When she put the bolt on my door, she nearly mentioned him. I remember *that*. Half his name slipped out, and I saw it floating in the air for days after. *Mar mar mar*, a little half story of a stain. I look at the air-purifying plants and wonder if they can purify that —all the words half said or regretted, swallowed up by reaching leathery leaves, returned as fresh air.

I fall asleep. There isn't anything else I have the strength to do.

I don't know long I've been sleeping for when I feel the gentle laying of a hand across my chest, long fingers pressing into my top, cool and dry, just beneath my collar bone. The pressure lifts me gently from sleep until I lie comfortable and warm in a fug of not-quite-awake, eyes closed, enjoying my Marty come so quietly to my room to wake me, our fight over and forgotten. He rests his hand where he can feel my heartbeat. He presses down, pinches gently at my skin. Gentle nibbling kisses start, around my neck, into the dip of my shoulder, down my arm. The nibbles become nips become bites and I wriggle with pleasure and reach to push his head down, and grasp a handful of dry, leathery leaves.

I must have screamed when I flung them from me, because Mam slams the door open, raging.

"What's going on!"

She sees the blood on the sheets, and my cut bicep, and the jointing knife.

The world becomes very loud and very small and very painful for a while.

When I open my eyes again, the knife is gone and the sheets are gone. There are plasters on my arm and the room is too warm. Mam's gone, but she's left a small plate with some cold pasta and tuna on it. Somewhere in the house, taps are running so the water rushing through the pipes carries her mutterings to me. She's muttering *about* me, and this is enraging. The rage raises me from bed, works my limbs with strings of hot righteousness.

I beat my fists against the door and shout, "I'm your daughter!"

I shout, "You can't ignore me!"

I shout, "It wasn't just me! He's lying, he wanted it."

And I know all of those things were true, at least once, but she doesn't open the door, and the pipes keep muttering, and eventually I'm left to sit on my bare bloody mattress and tremble and starve.

I pick the plasters off my cuts, the better to stop them healing. I open the window to let the air in, the better for the air plants to purify, and I sniff through the gap the delicious smells of the filthy street. My stomach starts wailing.

Then I notice Baby's missing from its sphere.

It's not gone far. I find it nestled by the foot of the bed, nearly blending in with the carpet pattern and the shadows. Pick it up carefully, resting it in my palm. It's still far smaller than it felt in my bed, but I'm sure its leaves are fuller, more succulent. Redder.

"You little Audrey," I murmur. I half admire the gall of it. My stomach is rumbling again, my sight blurring, and I'm astonished that even my own blood re-entering the body it came from can stir me so awake that the withdrawals have started again. I pet Baby, stroking its leaves, which are far more limber than they seemed. When it seems settled in my hand, I snap a leaf off, twisting it free. I fancy Baby bristles, but doesn't otherwise move. I chew the leaf and the flavour is green and red and good and I can swallow it easily, more easily than lettuce or tomatoes or boiled egg. Then the guilt twists again. "I'm sorry," I say, "I'm sorry." And I recall I've said that before, through a mouth full of blood and fatty meat, so I have to say it again. "I'm so sorry."

I must make amends. I lie on my bare mattress, and take Baby and place it on my cut bicep.

Nothing, at first. I close my eyes and turn my head away. Eventually I feel a tickling shift of the leaves as Baby adjusts itself, a careful nibble around the edges of my cuts. I look and see the wiry little pubic roots grasping the open red lines. Baby is nestling in, and its roots grasping and letting go, grasping and letting go. Its leaves waft slowly as though caught in a current, and I realise they are pulsing in time with my heartbeat. The feeding is utterly silent apart from my own breath, which comes faster and deeper the harder Baby pulls at my flesh. I see some of my blood trickle down into my armpit. A waste. Carefully, I scoop it up with the forefinger of my other hand, lick my finger clean.

Then I touch Baby. The feeding pauses. I fondle a leaf and then, to see what might happen, yank it. Baby clings to me, little root needles refusing to come loose this time, and the pain sears down my arm and I cry out, pull hard enough for the leaf to come free. I eat that one, too, stroking my hips and belly with my free hand. Consider the other plants.

When I stand, Baby stays put. So I unhook the spheres from the curtain rail and lie them on the bed next to me. I take off my t-shirt and lie down too. All through this, Baby feeds, and I notice its leaves have grown, new growth is appearing, long tendrils which whisper and reach and brush my skin. I lie on my back and close my eyes. I am still too hot, and now I am shivery, too, too sensitive, so I can't help but hear the faint clink of the spheres when the plants move. I hold my breath, waiting. Then the fingers come, the leathery leaves, gentle, probing and nibbling, reaching over my side, clambering onto my ribs.

Betty nestles into the dip at the bottom of my rib cage. Its leaves are dry and leathery, they scratch. They make me think of Marty's hands, his callouses. Further down, Biggun creeps along my hip. I touch it, and it stops moving. My fingers become wet, but I don't know whether they are slick with blood or sweat. I don't mind which. I lie there, and when I feel faint, I take a succulent leaf from whichever plant falls to my hand and replenish myself. Each time I pick a leaf, they are bigger, more swollen, and each time I think I'm full, my stomach aches empty again, and my limbs tremble and the plants grasp on more intently. They touch my nerves, they must, and I touch them, and we drink and drink, and I feel quite, quite beautiful.

It's quiet, apart from the rustling of the leaves and my breathing and my sighs and the murmurings from water in the pipes. Time passes, it must be passing, but all that marks it is the phone downstairs ringing. It rings and Mam doesn't pick up, so it rings and rings and rings. Then I feed to the rhythm of the ringing, frustrated when it stops, peaking and falling in an ecstasy of food, *finally* food—organic and orgasmic in a way I have been denied. Marty, I think, Marty you are missing so much. Marty, I only wanted a taste.

The phone rings, the phone rings, the water runs. In a final spasm of joy, my mouth full of plant fibres and blood, I roll on to the spheres and they break. The difference is in the quality of pain. The spheres are sharp, uncaring, screaming, and they bring me back to myself. I sit up and try to remove the plants from where they have settled. The crook of my neck, the back of my knee; Biggun's reaching leaves wrapped around my waist. They will not move. They refuse to let go. They want me. They need me.

The phone rings.

I pull at their leaves, without care, but the plants only cling harder, hotly red and rustling. If I had the knife, if I still had the knife, I would prise them free, but there's nothing in this room. I pull the bible from the drawer and use it to smack at Biggun and Betty as though they might shrink from the holiness, but the pages only become spattered with my blood and the plants don't budge. Like those seashells, I think, though the ringing keeps pushing the word I really want from my head, those pyramids, with the feet… the ringing the ringing. The limpets. I need to sit still and then take them by surprise.

The phone rings and the pipes gurgle and laugh. I sit and try not to tremor at the noise drilling through my head. After ten rings it stops, and I snatch suddenly at Betty and pull her from my leg. The bleeding screaming mouth she has left by my knee; the ragged holes and white of bone. I stamp on her and stamp until she is mashed and seeping. I do the same with Biggun and the heat of the air against my chewed waist makes me cry. I cannot remove Baby. It is too small, too nestled in and wet and feeding too hard. The phone starts up again.

I rush to the door and hammer on it.

"Mam!" I shout. "Mam, answer the phone. Answer the phone!"

But it stops only to start again. And stop and start and on and on and on and the door won't open. Did she say she was going out? I can't remember. She would have called Ellie to watch me, surely. I don't know. I am unsure—but also right! Because finally the ringing stops properly and it is replaced by the click of the front door opening and Ellie shouting "Hello! It's me!" Her voice is high and strained. I hear her hurrying through the house, but I don't hear Mam welcome her.

The taps stop running. The pipes stop whispering. There is shouting, and Ellie coming up the stairs, the clip-clop of the neat heels she likes to wear, and then she's at my door, *still* shouting, "Tannie, Tannie, are you there? Are you okay?" and fumbling with the lock.

I say, "I'm here." My voice sated and thick with satisfaction.

She thanks god and then swears and then says sorry to god, several times: *I'm so sorry so sorry oh god I'm sorry.*

I look down at myself, and realise what she will see when the door opens, but it's too late, and anyway, she loves me no matter what.

The bolt finally gives.

"Your mum, Tannis, your mum..." she says, as she pulls the door, and then she stops, and I watch her taking us in, me and Baby and my swollen blood-filled belly, and the broken glass and the mashed remains, and the handprints and the footprints where I rolled and moved and loved. The stained sheetless mattress.

I look at her looking at me, and I see the gobbets of blood on her chest where the necklace lay, and about her neck where the earrings swung. Divots and gobbets and spattering delicious mess, ripped and nibbled. Her blood smells sweet. It smells like dessert, or like takeaway when I only had my own boring tasteless dry toast self. She reminds me of the sweetness that was Marty, and my mouth waters, and I tell myself—*No, this is Ellie. This is my oldest friend.*

I wait for her to open her arms to hug me as she always does, but she doesn't.

She doesn't move at all, except her mouth. Her mouth opens wider and wider, spilling a loud noise into our small room. She can't move and she won't stop and the noise is not sweet—so we hug her instead, me and Baby, until she does.

The Waite People

Meg Elison

"MACHEN WAS at his peak in nineteen twenty-three," the talk began at the top of the hour. The speaker hadn't introduced himself, just wrote his name: Professor Ian Barrows, on one table tent and ARTHUR MACHEN in caps on the other that sat in front of an empty chair, as if the long-dead author were there in the room with him.

The speaker was a professor from a New England university. His seersucker suit was perfect for the unrelenting heat but rumpled by his perpetual slouch. He wore small circular glasses and a houndstooth bowtie. He ran his hands through his graying hair absently, constantly, as if what he really wanted to do was pull it out.

"And it was that year that he sent these newly discovered letters to his friend, the writer and occultist A.E. Waite."

Kate started texting her editor at *The Emerald Tablet* the second she caught on to what was happening.

hey

She'd had her phone in her hand so she could scroll while this guy talked through his usual circuit. Having read Machen her whole life, Kate had come to this panel on the final day of the convention just to kill time before her train with the barest hope that she might be able to wring an article out of it. At worst, the presentation was going to be yet another panel on "wasn't this old guy super great." At best, there might be something novel and exciting to talk about.

But Professor Bowtie had come out swinging with this. Kate shifted in her seat, leaning forward and thumbing up her notes app so she could take details down. New letters between Machen and Waite could mean a wealth of information on the two occultists: the author and the devoted mystic. This was better than she had bargained for, and she sharpened to it.

> hey I'm in this panel about Machen

She rushed to justify herself; making it clear she was not asking for his attention or to return to the endless dissections of how their affair had fallen apart. This was all business.

> looks like there's new manuscripts? Or at least uncut ones, from before that malted milk company made him edit out the sexy naked ritual scenes

After a few minutes, an answer came from Aaron, halfway across the country.

> shit, really?

Excited and relieved that he was catching her drift, she texted right back.

> I know, right? Sounds like an academic paper at least could be published next year. I'm staying in to see if I hear enough to write up the rumor, but it sounds like they discovered this stuff in Waite's papers.

> Waite? Like the Rider-Waite tarot deck?

The very same.

Looking up, she saw that the professor was plugging a projector into the port of his laptop, managing a dongle to make them come together.

I think there's an article in this for the Emerald.

Totally. Keep me posted!

"As you can see from this first document, Waite was very anxious for Machen to explain himself. He's more focused on what Machen discovered than what he wrote about it. That remains secondary."

The wild-haired Barrows got the projector focused, showing the Magician card from the Rider-Waite tarot deck.

"Though commonly referred to as the Rider-Waite deck, most scholars now call it the Rider-Waite-Smith to include the work of artist Pamela Colman Smith, who painted the images that have become the indelible face of the tarot as we know it."

He smacked the spacebar on his Mac and the slide advanced. Someone stood up and turned off the lights, unbidden. Kate looked over and saw their dark silhouette sinking back into a chair. She signed *thank-you*, her left hand glancing off her chin at the person who may or may not have seen.

The light in the room shifted away from the blue-white of the overhead fluorescent tubes and instead yellow shafts of muted sun came in through the half-covered windows on the far side of the room. The presenting professor was dark on his left and light on his right, continuing. In the strange new light, Kate caught movement out of the corner of her right eye.

It was common for her to see someone in the audience of a panel knitting, sewing or crocheting. Kate wasn't a fiber person and she didn't always know which of these things she was observing. This time, she was sure.

Limned in light, a person with thick forearms was spinning wool on a drop spindle just a few rows away. The ancient tool was silent and unobtrusive, but their rhythm was perfect. Kate saw the unblinking skill of the hand, rolling the spindle up the thigh clad in old, faded jeans, dropping and stretching again. Richly colored wool in green.

Looking back into her own lap, Kate thumbed on the comforting blue-white portal of her phone. No one had texted. Up on the screen, the prof was showing the Death card in a side-by-side with the Knight of Pentacles. The two images were essentially the same in shape and scale, but dressed differently and carrying a different object as they surged forward on horseback. Looking up at the cards, Kate realized she had touched both of them hundreds of times, never noticing they were twins.

"It is this queer doubling that Machen returns to, again and again. Waite assures him in their letters that this is the right road to go down, but urges him to skirt obscenity. And so the published versions of Machen's stories lack this particular ritual: the queer doubles doing their queer movements."

Kate texted to Aaron, suddenly needing a small laugh, though she knew not why.

> Only a prof of nineteenth century lit uses 'queer' to mean anything but 'gay'

But the professor was reaching a hand into the audience, toward the soundless person who had stood to turn off the lights. "If you'll help me, I believe I can demonstrate."

He slapped the computer again and the tarot cards were gone. In their place was a crudely drawn diagram; two stick figures in a series of gestures, like a dance. Their hands and feet were little slashes, but their angles were precise and equal. Tiny marks indicated their facial features, whether they were facing one another or away.

Aaron wrote back.

> Queer gestures

> That's the Machen thing, the way that bad geometry is Lovecraft's thing. You couldn't possibly imagine. It was so weird that it drove us all to madness!

Kate wrote back, not sure what she was saying.

Doubling

"Like this," the prof was saying, putting his hands up and being mirrored by his assistant. "This is somehow the rarest thing in all of Machen's work. This is what Waite was trying to preserve. The step-by-step description that always ended up cut from the final draft of the published tale. As if it were dangerous to tell people how these rituals actually went. As if he were trying to publish instructions, rather than stories."

The light in the room was darkening now, to that greeny-orange of the sky before a storm. Clouds were gathering around this little New England convention center; everyone had been expecting rain bad enough to rule out dinner on the patio. Inside, the effect meant that Prof. Barrows' assistant stood almost entirely in his shadow as they moved together in their mirror routine. Kate couldn't see the other person's face at all.

What's doubling?

I'm here in this room, and also with you

Sure, I see your avatar

Wasn't that the point of the internet? Being in two places at once?

"Machen insists in his letters, and Waite agrees," Prof. Barrow said, leaning over, his voice taking on the strain of strenuous movement, "that position is everything. Like the Death card. It's imperative to mimic these exact postures. One of my colleagues in another department suggested I compare this to the yogic postures, but I must confess I know little enough. And I rather think the two are unrelated."

The shadow of Prof. Barrow was much better at it now, moving soundlessly and unerringly with the person leading his dance.

"In Machen's masterpiece, *The Great God Pan*, we are given to understand movement as a form of prayer, of invocation. Many scholars who have come before me have ascribed to this a syncretic meaning."

To Kate's right, the spindle dropped and spun, dropped and spun.

Aaron, I am with you

typed her numbing thumbs.

Please don't start

came his answer.

"But as to why this would have been cut out by the editor at Horlick's, no one can say," Barrow went on. "Perhaps it was only a matter of length, to make room for an advertisement." Here, he joined hands with his shadow and they pulled one another into a kind of trick; a sliding lift like something swing dancers might pull off. But slowly. So slowly. Without momentum and against gravity.

To Kate's left, someone put up a hand and she was so grateful for a question to break this up that she almost hoped it was a long-winded fool with "more of a comment than a question." She was sweating, though the room was cold. Was it the pressure from the storm? The humidity?

But the hand that rose kept rising. Instead of hovering there, begging to speak, the hand took on volume and mass. She didn't want to turn and look. To her right, the spindle dropped and spun, dropped and spun. The sounds of chairs scraping against low Berber carpet. Two figures now, doubling each other, doubling Barrows and his partner.

"That's the spirit," Barrows said approvingly. "That's how we open the door."

From another conference room, Kate faintly heard music. Too early for the close-of-con dance. Was there a performance going on? That would be a good reason to leave. To open the door. To be elsewhere. And also here. The spindle dropped and spun.

Directly in front of her, two people rose. One wore a KN95 mask, the other an oxygen mask connected to a tank by a thin, clear tube. Unencumbered, the pair began to move and gesture and dance in exact sync with Barrows and his shadow.

Kate texted Aaron.

> Dance with me

She no longer cared that he was a former lover, that this might be taken as the resumption of affection, or as teasing about its lack. She needed a double.

> ????

> what is with you

Nobody else to dance with. An uneven number in the room. Just her, so odd. The person with the spindle was rising now, spinning still. The storm was gathering. Music, louder. What is that song? Thunder right behind.

Kate managed to text before she dropped her phone to the floor.

> Oh I am in trouble

She didn't know if she had hit the paper airplane to send or not.

"Come," Barrows said, his eyes glowing bright with orange-green storm light. He was a shadow now, too. "Come."

On the projector screen, a dim and fading image. The High Priestess, her foot cradled by the crescent moon. Enthroned alone. Uneven between black pillar and white.

Kate stood, not wanting to. Panicking, she mustered her strength. The lesser banishing ritual of the pentagram. The Swiss army knife of magick. She put her hand to her forehead, trying desperately to resist the tide pulling her toward Barrows. "Ateh," she intoned with all the strength she had left.

The spinner hummed loudly, picking up the song. It was not coming from another room.

"Malkuth," Kate said, her mouth dry as she touched her chest.

Thunder outside. Was the woman with the oxygen tank growling? Or was the oxygen running out? Was this happening? Or was a vein in Kate's brain messily bisecting itself? Her vision doubled.

"Ve-Geburah," Kate said, hands moving across her shoulders as if crossing herself. "Ve-Gedulah." Clasping her hands together, feeling her feet move without her. "La Ohlam, Amen."

"Yes," Barrows said, waving her forward to the light gathering in the front of the room. His disheveled hair standing up like the short antlers of a young deer. The smell of the storm. Petrichor and ozone. "That's right. Come, priestess. To the ages. To the ages, Amen."

To the ages, doubled together, they went.

Kate?

????

Seven Cups

Rebecca Kuder

[SUGAR EGG *(n.): an egg-shaped candy shell, often adorned with elaborate frosting, and a panoramic window. Through which to watch the scene inside.*]

TO MAKE A SUGAR EGG, first gather ingredients...granulated sugar, powdered egg whites, a splash of water. Forge a snowy, grainy dough to be molded, baked, and sculpted. A shell to be filled with tender, inert whimsy. Spring scenes, tufts of grass, and gamboling, downy beasts. Ducklings, hatchlings, rabbits. Innocent. But really, at its essence, a sugar egg is just a shell. And anything could be put inside, couldn't it? Anything could be painted, or pushed, or trapped inside. Something less comforting, more complicated than whatever sweet frippery the fortunate Christian children find in their baskets on Easter morning. You can make colored sugar paste and pipe sweetness around the edge of any opening.

A sugar egg could house just about anything.

Sweet or savory or something else, a sugar egg could house a story.

1.

I don't like people to stare at me. I don't show off at town hall dances, but there's something about you that I trust. Maybe because you're sitting there, attentive, ready to listen.

To follow each word.

Maybe because you want a secret, want to peek inside this fancy egg, where—if you hadn't slowed down enough to wonder— you might never know there's a whole sugared world, waiting, ready to discover. A quiet little secret world. Sparkly, candy-colored? Waiting in here. With me.

I can show you—can I show you? Bring your gaze to the sugar window. Look inside. If I say these words, you might glimpse something, a story, a quiet little secret, something that happened, a long time ago.

First: a house. Not stately, not fancy, but ample and solid, fine in its bones, secure, built with care and good materials. What seems a very pleasant house with clean windows and doors, something you can see inside, when the curtains are parted...and a lawn, the overarching impression of what you assume might signify calm, everyday, friendly comfort. Happy? A happy home. Nothing to indicate otherwise.

Holding, inside its cheery, framed shell, a mother and two daughters, eighteen and nearly twenty.

Sunshine. And in the sunshine, sitting in the front lawn...that's me. Having risen from the porch swing, having gone down the steps to sit in the yard...a hot day, the sun bright. Nearly too hot.

I wanted to peel off my dress and stockings and let the grass touch all of my skin, but that wouldn't have been right. That wasn't what we did, we of this amiable house, not me, not my older sister, mother, nor anyone we knew. The happy home and everything else in our staid, careful, wrapped-up-tight world made sure of it.

Mother raised my sister and me. Father wasn't discussed; he was barely a shadow, and if any of our neighbors knew or remembered, no one spoke of him.

Our town was built from *you should never*, and usually, we didn't do what we shouldn't. People stayed near their tended houses, took care of tidying, and worked at inconsequential pursuits. No one asked questions. Imagine a tree: we didn't branch far from the trunk. We stayed in lines that made sense, the only lines that had been permitted by earlier generations. *Do what they taught you. Don't smash things open, don't reach out or break out. Do what they say. You may sit in the sun, but don't make a spectacle. Keep urges under cover, inside. Hold yourself in.*

~

IMAGINE you're living in a house now that's a lot like mine. Friendly? Happy? See? You even have that porch swing, and those tender cross-hatchings, the trellis to obscure whatever, beneath the porch, may be hiding.

~

THAT SUMMER, so long ago when I sat on the porch of the happy house, or on the grass...any day...or for instance *that* day, the day in the grass when I wasn't ripping off my dress, just fanning myself and waiting for some wind to cool me: A gentleman strolled along the sidewalk, but did not stop at the lion.

People who passed sometimes lingered at the corner of our lawn because of the lion. A cast-iron lion, you could only see its head—the open maw—time-softened, emerging from the grass. People would stop, put a foot into the lion's mouth, make a wish. You had to find it for yourself, though, for your wish to come true. And it was easy to miss, if you weren't looking.

This gentleman passed our house—porch swing, yard—often that summer. He seemed friendly, attentive. Always tried to make me laugh. He said the silliest things, asked waggish riddles about zebras, giraffes, elephants. Sometimes my sister, when she could remove herself from work or the radio programs, would escape the house and sit outside in the world with me, and watch him. He performed tricks with his hat, this man—a straw hat, red ribbon tied and draping down the back of the crown. As if someone had forgot to trim off what was excess.

"Zebra elephant wants a treat," he said, and other nonsense, so silly...I believe his jesting brought me to trust him. He clowned with his hat, performed ridiculous dances, his movement angular, unfamiliar. Lithe in his summer suit, spirited and twinkly. Unpredictable. I watched him and so did others, neighbors sometimes watched...Sally across the way, and her mother...maybe each of us had singular thoughts about him, but everyone said *how witty and handsome. A gentleman,* they said, they could see, *even through the clowning.* A stranger, only in a temporary and paper doll way had he arrived at our town. People speculated, but no one knew.

Strolling past my house, tipping his hat. All his tricks. Again and again. That summer I sat on the porch sometimes, on the porch swing, occasionally mending something and talking to my sister, but more often alone, and he would pass. Act very unconcerned, completely at his liberty, tip his hat. Stop for a moment, act out his riddles and tricks. Make me laugh.

I wondered what was materializing in his thoughts, what hid beneath his amusement. *You know,* my sister said, *you can't quite trust a man like that.*

And yet after everything was swept and put away, and the inmates of our happy home had wished each other goodnight, I would lie in bed and pretend he was thinking of me. What would it be like to be alone with him, with time, and space? What had colored and shaped such a being?

Maybe because I often sat outside, watching the world, he chose me.

~

ONE AFTERNOON, I was on the porch hemming a tea towel, and he stopped at our house but didn't jest. Said hello directly, asked what I was doing. I held up the towel.

"Industrious," he said.

I laughed.

"That lion." He pointed at the lump of cold beast. "Tell me about it."

I said, "Put your foot in its mouth and make a wish. They say it might come true."

He approached the lion, pushed the toe of his shoe into its mouth, said some words I couldn't decipher. He looked straight at me and with his hands made the shape of a square, a frame. Said I looked very special. Asked if he might take my photograph, sometime.

"Some afternoon or other," he said. "In good light."

"Yes," I said, surprising myself.

His smile sent a shimmer through my ribcage. "Some weekend, once I'm back from the city," he said. He went to the city for drawing lessons, he said. He was an artist, said he could draw beautiful things with colored pencils, said some of them would make me blush. Said he had never had a live model, but he did have books, complete with helpful photographs. And he had a camera.

"No, I wouldn't dare ask a lady to shed her clothes just for my hobby," he said. He smiled then, showed his best charm.

When we made the plan—*I'll tip my hat, then you follow me to the streetcar*—there was a look on his face, a certain look. I still don't know what to call that look, but even thinking of it now brings on the shimmer.

And I wasn't sure I believed him about his models. He seemed like a person who would have no trouble peeling a lady from her layers.

AT OUR HAPPY HOME, I swept and folded and scrubbed and polished and beat everything. Made a show of coughing from too much dust. I told my sister and mother—in our house full of females—that the heat was defeating me. I splashed water at my temples to emphasize the point, finished chores as quickly as I could, and retreated to the porch. On the porch, I waited and waited.

2.

HE DID RETURN. He walked past, and looked at me, but this time didn't stop. He gave the signal and kept walking. I went inside and spoke a bouquet of lies to my sister and mother, and hurried the three blocks to the streetcar.

There he was at the stop, waiting for me. He smiled. My breath whispered through me like a sudden wind. I hoped no one I knew would see us, but soon the streetcar arrived and we got on. He found a seat for us near the back, and let me sit first. A breeze blew through the open window. On the ride, he asked me about myself. I told stories about my mother and sister, anything I could think of. He was different, on the streetcar, his posture stiffer. A man sitting nearby turned around and frowned at my friend's hat, then stared rudely back and forth between us, during the whole ride. Eventually we escaped that awful man, and disembarked in the center of town, near the apartment where he would show me his drawings and retrieve his camera. Impatient, busy people dashed from shops and jostled around us. I tilted my hat to shield my face, as if it was only the sun I was evading.

At his building, he opened the door and led me up three flights of stairs. At his floor, we leaned against the hallway wall, laughing, breathless together. He unlocked and opened the door. Removed his hat, pawed at his hair, and unveiled the crease at the corner of his mouth. His smile, his little charm.

"Well, it's not much," he said. One large room, a half-sized door in the corner, and such tall windows. The walls were decked with pinned-up things, sketches, cut-paper shapes, all manner of ephemera. Thick and buttressed with color, as if to keep the space warm, or muffle sound.

Never had I been in a man's room, and in truth, seeing all this was dizzying. Aside from these artistic effects, how few things he had. A primitive table, two chairs. A sink. A wardrobe, its doors closed. An easel. A narrow bed.

He washed his hands at the sink. His towel looked new, or clean. There was a remarkably tidy stack of newspapers, as tall as the wardrobe, somehow not toppling. He began the tour of his work.

Some of his pieces were sketches of industry, or nature...one was a portrait—of a polar bear! Many were his ladies, which, again, he swore had been inspired by photographs in books. He offered to show me the books. At first I declined, but he laughed at me, and pulled them from a shelf made from three crates. He turned pages and spoke quietly but with increasing urgency. Showed me everything. Bodies and parts of bodies, torsos bent and bending, parts spilling beyond the frame, but still so much to be seen, in shadow, and also in light.

He put aside the books. "Look at this." He turned an easel toward me. On the easel hung a perplexing drawing, which did not depict female bodies. A figure, shadowed and seen from behind, stood in the foreground, regarding the sky, the sky that was a shelf of clouds. The clouds supported seven dim cups. Each cup contained a different item.

❧

UNCANNY. All this detail you can see inside a sugar egg, can you believe it? If you look close enough. If you pay attention.

❧

INSIDE THE CUPS...

...a deity—a woman—her face a blue darker than the sky (*cerulean*, he said), hair coiled, eyebrow raised...

...a shrouded personage, standing but hidden under white cloth, arms outstretched, imploring—a red glow...

...a snake, rising, thin tongue licking...

...cerulean towers, an apex of manufacture, something *built*, not born...

...a trove of jewels and gold, overflowing...

...a laurel wreath crown, its open end pointing to the sky (as if to catch, or release), and on *that* cup's side, a shaded skull...

...and a cerulean lizard, claws curled round the lip of the cup, and its lizard tongue, thin like the snake's, licking the air...

And the central shaded figure, the watcher...an apparition? Receiver? Or conjurer? No. The figure's right hand seemed to tremble, to indicate surprise. Not manifesting, but startled, or warned...the lizard licking air, approaching the figure.

These unsettling symbols—harmless, I told myself. *Just colored pencils, on paper.*

He asked me what I thought, what I noticed.

"Your imagination," I said.

"Yes!" he said. "Yes. Sometimes I feel that's all we really have."

"Maybe so," I said.

"People say it's good to accumulate, but I'd rather breathe in all the air I can, the wind, your eyes," he said.

I looked away. Everything had broken open. This attention was too much.

"What's tempting you?" he asked, but I couldn't think how to say the feelings. I laughed, I don't know why.

His gaze vined through me. *The ants will crawl on my body, later, wait and see,* but first, he was ready to take photographs of me, he said. He retrieved a small suitcase, and his camera.

We rode the streetcar as far as we could. We were silent, feeling the wind. When it was time to dismount, he took my hand. We walked away from the streetcar, through a thicket of summer foliage, to a field he knew. Once there, he told me to get ready. I did—unbuttoned my shoes, rolled down my stockings, everything, just everything, until I was ready, and he told me where to sit. The grass prickled my bottom, warm, sharp. After a while, ants crawled on my legs and up my torso. I brushed them away when I could. He toiled, his camera—the bellows—reaching toward me. The silent music of its motion. He told me how to reposition myself, and I did, I did. I did what he said. We were far from everywhere else; we were on another planet, becoming what comes from fire, forging a new world. I trusted him. I signed the paper he gave me. I renounced my clothing and let the ants survey my terrain, let the sun torch parts of me that had never been exposed. It was humid that day, the air hazy. He took off his jacket and loosened his tie. The straw hat provided shade for his lens, his vision. The camera began to look alive, like it had a neck.

"Which cup do you choose?" he asked, from behind the camera.

"Why choose?"

"Which cup?"

Then I grasped what he meant. "The riches," I said, and he laughed.

He told me to act out each one, each cup in turn. From the suitcase, he pulled out props and supplies. He watched, gave orders, and when he was satisfied, took a photograph, and changed plates.

"Stop deliberating," he said. "There are no limits! Anything can happen, if we will ever stop interrogating our minds!"

Sometimes he took photographs between poses, said he wanted to capture motion.

I let him cover me with a shroud, and raised my arms, and did everything like he said, just so. I tried to stay still despite the sharp dry grass, the ants between my legs. Bodies adapt to their discomfort.

Even as he witnessed my earnest contortions, there was still something very far away about him, even when he came close enough that I felt his breath, close enough to bend my knee or twist my torso, push hair to cover or uncover my face. In undressing, I had also unleashed my braids, but I could still feel their tight coil on my scalp, that memory.

～

ALL OF THIS inside a sugar egg! Your time to peek! You get plenty for your money, so it seems.

～

HE WAS FAR from me even as he touched me. He wanted the photograph, and discarded, disregarded the tenderer parts of me, all that hid, quivered, inside the sugar egg of me.

As he took photographs of my seventh cup, where I posed as Lizard, he said, "Use your tongue."

And I did, I tried, I flicked it out and laughed.

"Keep going," he said. He didn't laugh. "Be blue."

I was unsure what he meant but tried and tried to lick air, tried to be blue—though he said he would tint the photograph, later—and flicked my tongue at him.

"Like this." He seemed angry, impatient. He demonstrated, lizarded all of himself out toward me. "It's quite hot, do you think I'm enjoying this?" he asked.

He licked and flicked and shimmered, and then very briefly, disappeared.

Very briefly.

"Did you see that?" he asked, coming back.

I didn't know what I had seen. A man behind a camera, the tongue of a lizard, he was gone. Had he gone?

I looked again and he was packing his equipment.

"Get dressed," he said.

He walked ahead of me, and I threw things on and rushed to catch up but he was too fast. I didn't know what to say as we waited for the streetcar. I straightened my clothing. When the streetcar came, he got on first, sat near the back. I sat near but not with him. In this awkward configuration, he accompanied me back to town, disembarking where—hours before—we had met.

Before he left, he said, "I'll be back. To show you the photographs."

I walked from the streetcar to the house, which had always seemed happy, but suddenly looked savagely blown open.

$\approx$

How DO you find your candy-view, thus far? Are you glad you looked? Are you curious about this secret? Is this faint wind soothing you?

$\approx$

HE HAD GIVEN me that paper to sign. He had called it a formality, so he could do what he wished with the photographs. I had never before signed a paper like that. He reassured me, showed me what to do.

After I had signed it, he thanked me and put it into his suit coat pocket. I knew the ink was still wet, would smudge; I knew it would be binding—bound me to the words, what I had agreed to, and done.

$\approx$

HE UNDRESSED me and captured me on film, and lizard-like, licked, and then disappeared...and reappeared. All this magic, how?

The secret you've been waiting for, inside the sugar egg, the secret you're peeping into my thoughts to discover: The secret is I wish even now that he had been intimate, been...fierce, even though what I can imagine, when I imagine, transgresses every-thing. I would have liked an opportunity, even there in the field on that unutterable afternoon. Even with the lizard. Liked to feel that candle-lick, feel the tender parts lit.

But after that day, he disappeared, perhaps to the city. I waited and waited but he wasn't there, wasn't walking past. The season changed. I put on a sweater, a blanket across my lap, curled tight into myself on the porch swing. Held myself in. But still my skin could feel the grass, the ants all over me and between my legs; I could see his lizard tongue, his disappearing, even as the autumn air rolled into my bones. Neighbors began to whisper about the man with the Venetian straw hat, who claimed to be an artist, with his tricks and colored pencils. They leaned together to knit their rumors. My sister heard whispers, talk, though how anyone knew for sure, I don't know.

When I thought of him, my body filled with uncertainty. As if there was something terrible looming, a storm. And he was some-where, outside, susceptible. I couldn't save him, how could I save him? He wasn't available to save, and anyway, save him from what? In summer, I lay in the disturbance of grass and tried to give myself over, let myself drown in the cups, all the cups, upended each one, spilled the contents to find what was inside, but his lizard tongue licked and he disappeared. He let himself fade, and I don't know where he went—I don't know how he wasn't there.

I thought he must have been frightened. Did he see something, when he had gone? Inside our sugar egg there's plenty to see, but was he somewhere else? Or is he still inside this egg with me? Still being watched, like his camera watched me, while you there watch whatever *you* can see through that fancy, crystalline gap.

His tongue was a flame. I know that much. His tongue was a lizard, and he was just gone. But he didn't let me understand. He never told me anything, never shared his reverie, his plight. Never shared his secret utterings, didn't say what he had wished for in our yard, with his foot in the lion's mouth. I wanted—if I'm completely honest, yes—I wanted the lick of him, the fire. That curl of a smile of his. His charm. I wanted him to disappear with my body, wanted to touch and be touched, wanted the fire to burn and essentialize me, wanted to be charred and tempered, made into glass, into stone. I wanted to see myself—just as you have, perhaps, seen me—as each of the seven cups, see my body torqued and twisted to depict his cups, the vision of the artist. To depict, maybe, his lion-wishes.

I wanted, I welcomed all this contortion. Needed it. Came alive with it.

And went to the city, to find—at least!—the photographs.

∾

You, there, looking: are you willing to follow me to the city? Will you pack a bag and come along? You are cordially invited. A delicate and postage-stamp sized backdrop inside the sugar egg changes, and you are watching, now, act three. If the first act is the happy porch and yard, and the second, the field full of cups, where that lizard disappeared. The city is the third.

Settle in now, please, for act three.

3.

Again I lied to my sister, my mother. It doesn't matter what I told them, I just arranged it so I could leave. Took an old carpetbag holding a few things. Walked bundled against the cold dawn to the streetcar, to go to the train. Direction? To the city.

—*Only once, when I was a young child, did Mother take Sister and me to the city. To view the winter shop displays. We rode the train, its rhythm both soothing and troubling. Looking out the window, up I held my sweet little doll to watch the world, all that was there and then gone—*

At the city train station, bumbling with no plan, I asked the station man where to find art classes. What a confusion of words I disgorged! But the dull man was busy and refused to help. I went out to the street and searched for art classes, walked and walked, sought a building like the one in the photograph tacked to his overflowing wall, a picture postcard someone had made of smartly dressed students, painting and drawing, which he had proudly shown me, *Here's the school,* but every building looked just like its neighbor and all blurred into jumbled masses of brick and stone, and sometimes people growled at me when I asked for help.

(Inside the egg, this third act backdrop, I admit, is torn and grimy in places: coal clogs the air from industrial pioneers' years of pushing through hills, grinding substances at stoic factories, day after day.)

It was cold, the city, and I was growing hungry. I found a sheltered place to sit, a bench on a public square between buildings, where city pigeons pecked dirt and quarreled. I unwrapped the dry lunch I had brought and ate it, quickly. In the city, no one noticed or cared about me.

Again I walked.

The city's low river licked the banks like a lizard tongue, and for a moment I felt invisible, as if I, too, had disappeared, conjured by the river's lizard lick.

I walked and walked. It grew dark and I thought I saw him from behind, and I called out, but no, the stranger turned and startled me with a different face. With the few dollars I had, I stepped inside a greyish dining house, all steamy and meat-scented, but at least warm. A large man steered me to a stool at the counter, because I was just one. A girl behind the counter poured me a cup of coffee, brought food. But soon they needed my place, and it was impolite not to go. I set off for the train station, and there I bundled onto another bench, and maybe I slept.

THE WATER...IS the sky, my...body is submerged under rocks and sand, upside down and holding the grandest cup upside down, keeping it underwater...the cherubs beneath my head are drowning, holding their breath, even the mermaids...all we can do...we are each, all, holding our breath. The stones above my feet are endless, smooth, round, varied. The cherub above my seat is reaching, pushing me down, holding me under the sky of water, *where are the clouds?* I don't know how to breathe, and I won't give up, but I haven't yet found my way toward daylight, toward the air, don't yet know how to survive. I study the grand cup and focus my imagination on its intricacies, how the cup might help me...its handles are the claws of a crab, this cup...this cup of a sea creature is all I have. I will have to follow this sea creature up toward light, and air, if that's where it goes, will follow this cup, this crustacean, in order to survive.

And yet, *Beauty!*—I find—I can breathe. *If I am a lizard, then the water is the sky, and underneath, there is air.* I have to gasp, and risk living, to learn that the air has been here all along.

AN UNSAVORY EGG, a rotten egg. Covered in candy gloss but rotten even before it was adorned. Who *made* this egg? Shell blown out, but still with licks of albumen, still maybe a dot of red, can you see it? Evidence of former life. Do not eat this egg. The sugar bits, the crystals and shards through which you gaze are cracking, and under the façade of cloy you can smell, if you breathe in, and close your eyes, how things have turned, that saline, that bit of stench.

~

DON'T LEAVE ME, I said aloud, waking in the dim train station, my shoulder sore, prickling with pain, and my coat not warm enough. Who was I telling?

~

IT'S appalling but I don't know how I got home. Nothing in my bag. No photographs, not having found my body's contortion of cups. Not having found the man. At home, they cooed and curred over me, after first roaring their fear and heartache. Sister slapped me, Mother cried, collapsed. But even with their theatrics, still— they were far away. I was there, alone, in the bathtub, warming my shivered skin, but also I was gone, back somewhere in the city, or in the field, a lizard, like him.

~

HE WASN'T RICH, no, not rich, in fact we heard he died without enough for burial, that's what my sister said, that's what she *heard,* if what my sister heard can be trusted. Sometimes I just don't know. He died too young, he was too tender and broken for how things are, how you just have to settle down and make a way for yourself. How you have to be sensible. Have to hold yourself in.

But my sister heard he had hanged himself, alone in a small hotel room, his suitcase, colored pencils, some personal papers. A camera. Some undescribed photographs. A life in flux, then a life fixed. If death is as stagnant as it seems. He didn't have anybody, and certainly no one to write his obituary, no tribute to his shameful, magnificent drawings, his crease, that tiny charm he carried on his face, that place of lizard lick, at least what he showed to me.

~

A CANDY EGG that has rotted, is rotten. Cracked open, on purpose, with a window whose only point is to reveal, to allow violation. A vista for spies. You are complicit. The shell opens. Opens, and inside that's no fluff-wet chick, no, nothing sweet and frail. Opens, and instead of a baby bird's translucence, behold the gore: see a snout, cold, spotted, scaled, see its tongue, licking, flicking at air, an egg opens and offers not soft down but cold blood, mineral, something that, nevertheless, sees many things, sees and makes beauty and sees a girl, *sees me*, bends me into so many cups. A flicker appearing only to disappear.

~

THAT MAN, that lizard never did and no one *ever* in my whole life gave me a chance to delve into decadence more than what I agreed to enact in the field, and I wish he had, I sure wish he had.

~

SOMETIMES, I dream, and dream the sugar egg, with its rotten bits still clinging, dream the sullied egg isn't an egg, but a cup, that contains something wild, unknowable, something living and not, something here, something gone, a puff of smoke, a memory, a life, dangling from the rafter, a body, stripped yet *trying* in the violent grass of the ever after. Something dead. Something alive, now. At least something. You are complicit. And all because you, in your endless patience, have watched, have imagined it all uncurl...

No Light in The Trees

John Patrick Higgins

THE COLD REMINDED her of her bones, the stiff scaffold propping her up. She felt dense and heavy, only the stone-hardness of the earth keeping her from sinking into it. Shuffling from side to side, knees grinding like gears, she watched Greg wipe condensation from the monitor. Daisy squeezed her arms and chest, trying to pinch the cold from her body—hot pain offering sharp relief. She'd be a mess of bruises by morning.

It was the second day of broadcast, and the old trouble was bubbling up again. Steve had been talking over her on camera. It was always the same: the bristling machismo, the chippy put-downs, the constant one-up-man-ship. Where did it come from? He was a *bird spotter*. He spent his free time squatting in hides with other misfits, jotting down bird names in Latin, but put a camera on him and suddenly he was Jason Statham. Daisy respected Steve's knowledge—he was encyclopaedic, and everybody knew it, he *needed* them to know it—but she had a BSc in Zoology from the University of Reading, so she knew her mustelids from her ungulates. Besides, she was younger and better looking, and many of the viewers preferred her. Steve could be awkward and say strange things if he went off-script.

She'd taken it up with him over dinner, and of course Steve claimed ignorance and was hurt by the idea. He imagined he was as generous a co-presenter as he was a lover, which led to a smirk and then an argument, and the atmosphere remained frosty on set the next day. But he'd let her finish her pieces to camera without any of the usual heckles.

But the interruptions returned. Daisy shook her head and gave her rueful smile and the occasional, "When you've quite finished, Steve…" and the viewers thought this was chemistry, the funny way they rubbed against one another: Steve incorrigible and puppyish, Daisy stern but indulgent. Their audience of *Daily Express* readers enjoyed this as though it were the natural order of things: boys will be boys, after all. Behind the scenes things were poisonous: slanging matches and slammed doors. In one regrettable incident a polished kestrel's skull was crushed beneath Daisy's heel, and there was almost no coming back from that. Eventually, she apologised, replaced it, and uneasy peace was restored. It was surprisingly easy to get hold of a kestrel's skull. You just had to know the right people.

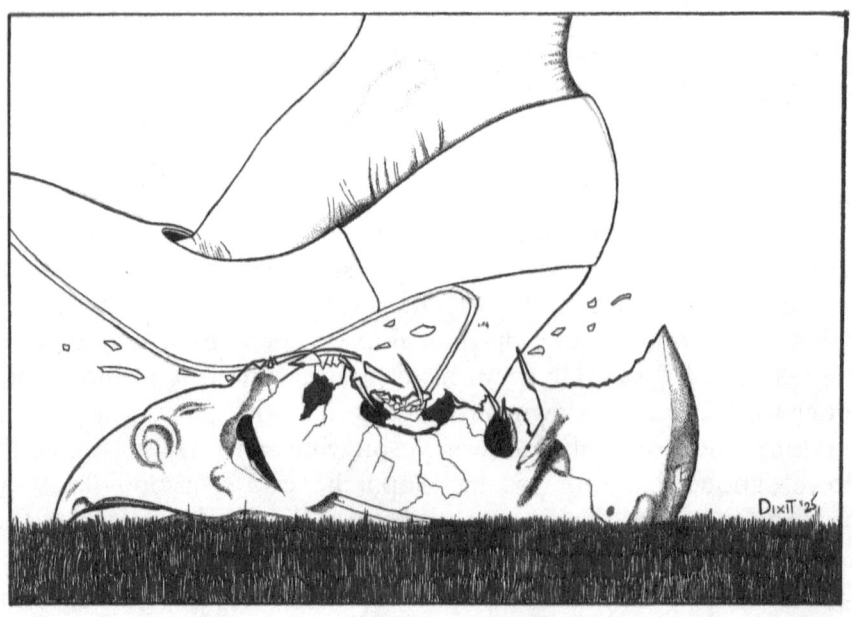

"You really like the murderers, don't you?"
Steve popped a forkful of meat into his mouth and registered

the comment with a raised eyebrow. They were in a quiet restaurant. It was late and Steve ordered his steak *bleu*. Blood dripped down his chin. Daisy twirled some gnocchi in a cheese sauce and looked away.

"If you're asking whether I prefer predators to prey, then yes. It's the aesthetics on one level. Look at those larger predatory birds: they're beautiful. But it's also the engineering. They're glorious machines, perfectly honed for finding and dispatching prey."

"They *do* have excellent talon/eye coordination."

"I think you're trying to be funny, Daisy," (He was never sure.) "But you're right. I much prefer these active, entrepreneurial animals to your twitchy-nosed accidents-waiting-to-happen. You must admit there's something sexily proactive about going out there and taking what you want. What you need to survive."

Daisy dabbed her lips with a napkin.

"You should be on *The Apprentice*, Steve. *Entrepreneurial animals.* You sound like a loon."

She scraped her chair back and got up to go to the bathroom.

"Wrong actually," Steve called across the restaurant, "this is what a loon sounds like."

And he proceeded to do an accurate impression of the North American aquatic bird. The other diners looked on concerned, until they realised Steve was off the telly, after which they thought it was quite good.

TODAY DAISY WAS ALONE on the outdoor studio set, while Steve was away in Pembrokeshire filming a dead badger. Carrion animals were coming from miles around to devour it, species of every size efficiently levelling the corpse. That was nature. It was clean, it was democratic, it left nothing behind and, once it'd been broken down, the earth would devour the animal remains and it would foster new life. Steve never bothered with that bit. He was only interested in the ripping, the tearing, the harm. He liked the hook-beaked birds with their sickle claws, he admired their special adaptations, the silence of their soft wings, their unblinking yellow eyes. The fast, furry things they ate were just fodder necessary for the upkeep of these magnificent animals, palpitating bundles of nutrients to keep their feathers shiny and sleek. Steve loved it out there in the darkness with his killer friends.

~

"I've seen them all," said Steve.

"All of what?" said Daisy. She lay on her back, the ashtray resting on her chest. The banquette in Steve's trailer was surprisingly roomy.

"All the big predators."

Daisy raised herself onto an elbow, ashtray cupped in her hand. "That's where your head's at—the scary monsters in the woods? This is your post-coital chat?"

"Not just the woods, and not just this poxy country either. I've seen them all: *Carchadon Carchais*, *Harpia Harpyja*, *Ursus Maritimus*: all that strength, that poetry, that magnificence."

"Ursus…? Where did you see a Polar Bear?" Steve shifted his weight and dropped cigarette ash onto his thigh. He massaged it absently into the skin.

"It was a zoo, admittedly. And it looked depressed and a bit mangy. But it was still awe inspiring."

Daisy sat up, pulling the blanket with her.

"We're killing them. Polar Bears are out there floating around on surfboards of ice. That second one—the harpy eagle, was it?"

He nodded.

"We've destroyed its habitat. It's dying out. These sexy super predators aren't really much cop when they come up against humanity, are they? We're the meteorite that killed the dinosaurs."

Steve sat forward on the banquette, naked but for his Y fronts. A cigarette dangled at his lips.

"You're right. We've turned an ecological corner, despite what Attenborough reckons. I think they're just hiding the facts from him so he can die happy. The Anthropocene is crushing life on this planet like a digger through the rain forest. All we can do now is record them before they disappear. But I would just like to find one, just one."

"One what?"

"Something human proof. Something we couldn't hurt, something new—the apex predator of planet earth."

"It's right here, Steve," said Daisy, "and it's smoking in its underpants."

There were more skirmishes on set. Daisy had decided to stop sleeping with Steve and Steve had taken it badly. He didn't *care*—he didn't particularly like Daisy, but he'd enjoyed the sex, and it helped him sleep. Daisy didn't care either. She'd slept with him out of boredom while they were on location. It was something to do. It kept her out of the hotel bar and was marginally less tedious than a static bike. It pleased her now not to sleep with him, to watch him pout and fuss, to throw things around in the production office. He'd tried to get her sacked, she knew that. They wouldn't fire her. She was becoming popular. Someday she'd be more popular than Steve. He was limited and self-sabotaging. He couldn't think on his feet, and there was something else…snobbery. He thought the programme was beneath him, he should be doing more important things. The audience had started to pick up on it.

STEVE WAS DOING his piece to camera, intercut with night-vision footage of pine martens ransacking the corpse. Everything was camouflage green except the animals' glowing eyes, ghostly and phosphorescent from the imperfect technology.

Steve's eyes were wet and white too, poached eggs on the green plate of his face, as he enthused in near darkness ten feet from the corpse. Daisy, warming her hands around a machine coffee, watched the monitor through clouds of breath. Steve would soon cut to a lengthy film about sheep, introduced by a farmer who had fluked a telly gig. There would be ample time to finish the coffee while the farmer took the camera crew on a tour of his barns, lovingly fingering his feed barrels, patting the shining flanks of his tractors. He was a very boring man, a flat cap and red trouser Tory, and perhaps more casually sexist than Steve. His rosy-cheeked, hearty wife was worse. They were back slappers and common-sense enthusiasts, and they went to bed early.

Daisy frisked herself down with her free hand. Did she have time for a crafty fag? Did she even have any? Steve had finished his opening piece, and the farmer filled the screen with his lipless pink face. The live feed continued alongside it, and she could see Steve on the other monitor, clapping his hands together and doing star jumps to keep warm. He looked like a child in his big puffer jacket. It was almost endearing.

She had no cigarettes, so she drew the coffee to her lips. It was already getting cold. There was an odd flicker on Steve's monitor. Something behind Steve moved. Just for a moment. Something shifted in the dark. She squinted at the screen. Nothing. Just the night. Then again…there…a sudden ripple in the darkness, black on black, the difference only described by movement.

"Rosie?"

Rosie, the director, plodded over, looking flushed and harassed, as she always did.

"Everything okay?" she said. "You're on in three, so you might want to toddle over to your mark, please, Daisy."

"I think there's something…there, on the monitor. There's something moving in the background where Steve is."

"Is it something good? Is it a bat? A bat would be great. We haven't had a bat in ages."

"It's not a bat. It looks…big."

Rosie squinted. "I can't see anything."

"No, it's gone now, I think."

"Okay, well if you could just shrug off your blanket and hit your spot, that would be great."

"How am I for shine?"

"Lovely matte finish, darling…Oh God, are you wearing your poppy? Twitter will *crucify* us."

Daisy flashed her buttonhole and practiced her smile. Her teeth dried under the lights. The prompt was cued, and she snapped into action.

"Fascinating trip round Phil's seed bins, there. You think you know the half of it… Now, it's back to Steve, stumbling about in the dark and staring at dead bodies—just a normal Thursday night for you then, Steve?"

There was the usual awkward satellite delay before Steve replied. "Ha, yes, very good, Daisy. I *could* tell you about my Thursday nights but then I'd have to kill you. One feller who won't kill you—he'll wait till you're already dead—is this silphid beetle, *nicrophorus humator*…"

He was off again. Daisy could stop smiling. Her cold face sank by increments, cheek muscles stiff, intractable. Rosie rushed up to her.

"You're right! Twitter's gone mad!"

"I'm *wearing* it."

"Not the poppy, the *thing.* Loads of people have seen something large and dark moving about behind Steve. It's getting loads of traction. We have to play it up—this sort of thing is numbers magic."

Daisy knew something that Steve didn't—this could be a chance to shine. She would be fed the viewer's comments and, crucially, it was happening behind Steve's back. He had no idea what was going on.

"Steve," she said, "sorry to interrupt, but you seem to have some sort of visitor."

"What?" said Steve, failing to hide his annoyance. A point to Daisy.

"Viewers have been texting in to say you're not alone. They've seen something mysterious lurking about behind you. Ruth in Taunton says, "There's something big and black moving about in the shadows behind Steve." And Russ19—doesn't say where he's from—tells us, "There's something weird happening behind the dead badger. The trees are shaking." What d'you think Steve? Are you getting any weird vibes?"

Steve looked over his shoulder and returned to camera.

"Sorry to say my Spidey sense is *not* tingling, Daisy. Nothing unusual out there as far as I can see. Wind's picked up a bit, so I'm getting a fair whiff of badger, but there's nothing else going on here. Sorry about that."

Rosie was in Daisy's ear, and she reacted in a split-second. She was a pro.

"We've got some footage, Steve."

The screen filled with blurry, greenish landscape, white lights picking out the pine marten's eyes, the degraded stripe along the badger's nose, and a couple of shiny-backed insects. Behind this a couple of ghostly trees shivered against the inky permanence of the distant woods. A suggestion of smeary white clouds high in the frame.

"I don't see anything," said Steve, "couple of pine…."

In a second both pine martens had disappeared, too quickly for the cameras to pick up.

"Smell's getting stronger," said Steve, "odd. Carrion usually has a very distinctive odour...."

"You getting top notes of tonka bean, Steve?"

"If you'll let me finish, Daisy," said Steve. His voice was clipped, his face tight. He didn't like interruptions, and his mask of affability had dropped. Daisy allowed herself a quick smirk.

"It's not like any dead badger I've ever smelled—leave it...it's muskier, heavier. I don't know. There's something like cut grass or compost, but stronger...what—*is* it?"

Steve froze. A low growl was audible. At first Daisy thought it was a technical fault, but the noise persisted. It was clearly animal. You could hear the throat in it, something wet, meaty. The night sky was flattened, dead, and she thought the stars were hidden behind thick cloud, but now it looked almost as if some part of the night sky had broken off, fallen away. Her eyes tried to focus on the sudden, shifting darkness, but it was too hard to look at. It made no sense. Her bearings were lost. She focused on the show's host instead. It was easier.

Steve, looking wildly about, grabbed a part of the lighting rig, and sent the spotlight on a mad dance across the trees, exposing only pale nests of detail. Nothing but bushes, scrub, etiolated grass and the hollow outline of a dead badger, lying in the dirt.

"I thought I saw something, Steve," said Daisy.

"What was it? I can't see anything. There are weird sounds... and the smell, the smell is just...."

"I can't tell. It's too dark. The cameras can't pick it up. We're just getting lateral signs."

"What does that mean? Talk sense."

"We can't see a *thing*, but it does look like...there..."

Steve lurched round, arms wide. He seemed to have heard something but whatever it was was lost to the audio.

"Is that...hello? Hello? Who's there...is that..." The audio stuttered, and Steve bolted towards the darkness, stumbling over the grey-green fuse and to the trees. The sound picked up fractured dialogue, as the cameraman and soundman wandered into shot, ghost faced. Chris, the boom operator, was talking over the camera, but the conversation was intermittent, stuttering. Both technicians disappeared behind the static camera, and it jolted back into life, following Steve into the darkness.

He was running up and down over the hollow where the dead badger lay, still waving his light about like a will-o'-the-wisp, illuminating the filigree of the foliage, the detail of the trees' bark.

And he found it.

There was a patch where the light would not take, where there was either nothing for the light to show, or something light couldn't describe.

Steve had his back to camera now, and was staring off into the emptiness, the light in his hand finding nothing until, faintly, and with luminosity unrelated to Steve's torch, two milk-white lights appeared, high over the ground. There was a crackling noise, and the audio finally sputtered out, breaking up into silence. Daisy could barely see the two hazy spots of white. Initially they seemed fixed, but slowly drifted apart, flaring with milky luminescence, and she realised with a jolt she'd misread what was happening. They *were* fixed points, because they were eyes, eyes staring through the darkness, and they weren't flaring, they were moving closer, closer to the camera, closer to Steve. Beneath the eyes, just for a second, was a sudden slash of white through the black night, a tick of chalk on slate. The ghost of a smile searing like an optical glare. The eyes were clear and tightly delineated now, hard and white and whole. Nothing misted the edges, nothing softened them. Daisy shuddered. Whatever it was, pushing through the dark toward Steve, wasn't breathing. Or its breath was very cold.

Rosie was shouting in her ear as Daisy screamed, but Steve could no longer hear them. His misty breath haloed over his right shoulder as he moved away from the camera.

"Steve, what are you doing?"

"Cut to the owl footage," yelled Rosie in her ear. At the bottom of the screen tickertape of viewer's panicked texts scrolled, as Steve staggered into the darkness. At some point he raised his arm as if to fend something off— or horribly, as if to take its hand. His own hand disappeared, pinched off at the wrist and, for a moment, he seemed to hesitate. He turned back to the camera. He was crying, and even though it didn't make sense, Daisy was sure he was grinning, his teeth flaring in the cold light. Was he saying something? His lips moved and he appeared to repeat the same two words, three or four times, perhaps, and with his remaining hand he pointed upwards and gestured about him. He was really laughing now, the tears wet on his cheeks, so they glowed, his eyes empty white discs, cat's eyes.

He turned back to the darkness. One last plume of breath hung gently in the air, and he was gone. The camera joggled, and Daisy could see the boom operator running across the woods, his microphone in both hands. Steve was gone.

The wind stopped and there was silence and stillness. Just the film crew, crossing backwards and forwards in front of the camera, out of focus. There was nothing: beyond the canopy of the trees, beneath the empty, starless sky. There was nothing. Only darkness, only the night. The owl footage played, slightly too late.

Alone in the studio, Daisy stared into the camera. The owl story ended. Rosie was silent in her earpiece. Daisy's eyes were burning with cold tears. The microphone felt a part of her, a part of her arm. Dead air, just for a second.

Daisy heard herself saying to camera: "Sorry about that—we seem to have lost Steve there."

The Macabre Reader

Lysette Stevenson

THE TREE of Sacrifice BY PER FAXNELD. Illustrated by Mimmi Strinnholm. Translated from Swedish to English by the author for *Egaeus Press*, 2024.

Set in the early to mid 1800s in a rural region of northern Sweden, *The Tree of Sacrifice* contains forty-four disquieting tales. Here we meet people in a pre-industrial world, whose old gods and superstitions are an integral part of their day-to-day lives. Christian missionaries have yet to reach these villages and the things that live in the shadows have a different world view. These vignettes are not morality plays like the lessons of Aesop's fables; there are rituals outsiders will not understand and areas one never passes in the woods. As each tale is often met with a gruesome demise, this is folk horror through and through.

They are addictive and wholly original to the author but read like they could have been passed down through the generations. I found myself on a stormy autumn afternoon unable to put the book down, entranced by these stories of witchcraft and cunning folk, of dark and mysterious Swedish woodlands and their inhabitants.

Each of the forty-four tales are strikingly illustrated by Mimmi Strinnholm's black and white prints. In the Afterword, Faxneld encourages the reader that they are meant to be shared aloud. Passed around at a gathering, keeping the oral tradition of story-telling alive. Followed by a night walk in the woods to listen for what you might have stirred up.

～

HARVEST RITUAL: A SCREENPLAY BY LUCIO HOLOCAUSTO & KILLJOY. Cover art by Colin Rodgers. *Death Wound Publication*, 2020.

Set in a small town in the United States, our protagonist, Aelistra, is a malcontented goth teen seeking something bigger in life. Meanwhile, a rash of satanic murders sweeps not only their community but the nation at large. The town priest is mysteriously given an old grimoire; by studying it he hopes to uncover who the cultists are and how to stop them. This is a thoroughly cinematic read; the scene directions are as compelling as the dialogue and the narrative drives forward with nary a misstep. An homage to Italian film director Lucio Fulci's *Gates of Hell Trilogy*, with gore as surprising as it is inventive. It melds American era satanic panic, Manson cultists and a plethora of easter eggs for underground metal fans. This is splatterpunk written for horror metal maniacs.

Harvest Ritual, began as a short story/fan letter in 1999 by Doc "Lucio" Holocausto to Frank "Killjoy" Pucci, lead vocalist of *Necrophagia* and one of the founding fathers of American Death metal. Killjoy turned it into a creative partnership. As co-writer,

Killjoy presented Holocausto with sketches of brutal imagery. Holocausto reworked his story into a screenplay between the years 2002 - 2004 while completing his doctorate in English. What was to be Killjoy's directorial debut was never actualized due to his untimely passing in 2018.

Warning to the curious, I have only read the sold out first edition. The latest, expanded edition by Evilspeak Productions, includes deleted scenes, which were deemed too extreme for the original print run.

∿

THE NECRONOMICON: The Book of Dead Names EDITED BY GEORGE HAY. *Corgi Books*, 1980.

The dreaded Necronomicon, a ruse to this day that still has people questioning the legitimacy of its origins. Picking up where H.P. Lovecraft left off with his 1938 text, *History of the Necronomicon* and carrying the tradition set forth by Lovecraft's circle, George Hay pulls together a compelling essay collection for the Mythos. His contributors devise a narrative that Lovecraft's father was an Egyptian Mason, giving him access to a portion of an ancient Arabic text titled *'The Book of Secret Names'* and *'Of the History of the Ancient Ones.'* Here they convince the reader that young Howard was exposed to the text, infecting his imagination with nightmares and opening the gateways to horrors that lie beyond this world.

Colin Wilson's essay claims he has no intention of making the readers' "flesh creep," but that is exactly what he does. The hoax was so effective, after its publication they had to continuously disclaim that it was an actual scholarly work. Adding to its authenticity the text is accompanied by eldritch sigils and illustrations from occultists, Gavin Stamp and Robert Turner. Angela Carter's essay on "Lovecraft and Landscapes" is worth the price of admission alone.

I've encountered many earnest conversations, either in our bookstore or with a friend, that the true book of the Necronomicon is, in fact, fiction. As decades of lore, art and cinema build up around it, the debate persists. George Hay's collection is a fun, albeit creepy, contribution to the legacy of this mythos.

～

PASSAGE TO THE DREAMTIME: a one-act play BY ANYA MARTIN. Illustrated by Kim Bo Yung. Number Two in the Dunhams Manor Playhouse series. *Dunhams Manor Press*, 2017.

A young cabaret singer visits her former lover in his jail cell after the Nuremberg trials to tell him she bore his son. During their affair she only knew him as a German artist living in occupied Paris. After the trials she learns he was a high-ranking general who committed atrocities. She grapples with this revelation, that the man she loved and now has a child with, is not who she thought he was. While he recounts his crimes to her and loses his grip on reality. Through this heightened state they enter an alternate dimension.

As a stage manager, I find the ideas of weird fiction intersecting with theatre intriguing. Even more so when it's a highly charged one-act like Anya Martin has written here. Reading a play requires a mental shift. It's up to the reader to fill in the blank canvas the playwright has provided, imagining how it will be staged. Engaging creatively with the work is a rewarding exercise. Despite Anya writing this play years before it was first published, it is a prescient one-act, as we witness history repeating itself with the rise toward authoritarianism in the western world today.

Passage to the Dreamtime, is also available in Anya's excellent debut collection, *Sleeping with the Monster*, published by Lethe Press, 2018.

～

AGAINST THE LIGHT: A Nightside Narrative BY KENNETH GRANT. Cover art, Steffi Grant. *Starfire Publishing*, 1997. Second printing, 2016.

British author and occultist, Kenneth Grant, was notorious for blurring the boundary between fact and fiction in his writing. *Against the Light*, is at once a fictional pulp adventure and an ambiguous esoteric account of Grant's personal life. Grant is the protagonist, along-side real-life friends and associates: the magus Aleister Crowley, author Sax Rohmer and artist Austin Osman Spare. Combined with references to fictional characters from work the likes of Arthur Machen and H. P. Lovecraft.

While exploring his genealogy, Grant encounters an ancestor from the 1600s who was executed for witchcraft. Through this he discovers there is a Clan grimoire. He enlists the help of a scryer to seek out where this book has ended up. Dark forces are unleashed either due to the investigation into the book's whereabouts or from the scryer drawing up their energies. Once the grimoire is found in a Welsh crypt, the veil between the waking and unseen world thins. It becomes a race against time to stop the evil forces that are descending upon humanity. Time travel, dream logic and stream of consciousness take over the narrative. This melding of real and unreal creates a dizzying experience for the reader, heightening the weird with uncanny revelations as you embark on this journey with him. The line between what is actually a magical working or surre-alist pulp fiction, is up for the reader to interpret.

～

BLOOD BY HANS HEINZ EWERS. *Valcour & Krueger*, 1977. *Edition displayed, Heron Press, 1930. Lithograph by Edgar Parin d'Aulaire.

Subtitled by the publisher "Three Tales of the Ultra-Cruel" this collection lives up to the name with three stories drenched in carnage. "Mamaloi," is narrated by a German merchant living in Haiti at the turn of the century. Written through diary entries and letters, detailing his depraved exploits and participation in Voodoo rituals and sacrifices, all meant to torment his religious brother back home. The next story, "The White Maiden," looks over a gathering of bohemians, dining and anticipating a soon to be revealed magic trick. A radiant young woman materializes before them while grotesquely tearing apart a living dove. The final story, "Tomato Sauce," involves a cock fighting ring that progresses from roosters to men brandishing knives, presided over by a vampiric pope. This collection is proto-splatterpunk a la the Grand Guignol. Ewers' style of shock arouses all of the senses with a level of fascination and eeriness that is impossible to shake off.

Ewers was a decadent horror writer between the wars, considered the German 'Poe' of his era and an influence on H.P. Lovecraft. Despite being a prolific writer, his reputation is mired in controversy. He joined the National Socialist party in 1931 but he was promptly rejected for not only being bisexual but for protecting and aiding in the escape of his Jewish friends. By 1934, his works were banned by the Nazi party and labelled as 'Degenerate Art.'

❧

GRAVE DESIRE: A Cultural History of Necrophilia BY STEVE FINBOW. Illustrated by Karolina Urbaniak. *Infinity Land Press*, 2024. First publication Zero Books, 2014.

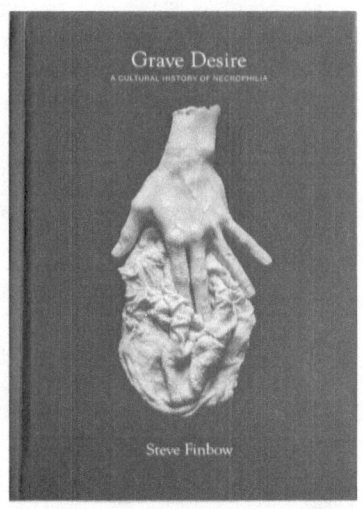

Illustrated and expanded, Infinity Land's reprint of *Grave Desire* is a critical examination of how a human comes to fetishize the dead. The transgression of necrophilia is so extreme, accounts of it throughout history have often been attributed to supernatural creatures. Ghouls disinterring a freshly buried body, werewolves desecrating a corpse in primal lust, or vampires ravishing with murderous appetite. As if, the preternatural is easier for our mind to comprehend than a human grave-digging for sexual gratification.

Finbow's narrative style is deadpan, he reels out the data and facts in a way that rarely feels salacious despite the subject matter. That said, the details are overwhelming and you begin to feel like necrophilia might not be as rare as you would like to believe. Interspersed are quotes from works of fiction like Poppy Z Brite's necrophile romance *Exquisite Corpse* and Bret Easton Ellis's serial killer satire, *American Psycho*. Attempting to understand what drives the necrophile and what repulses the rest, he explores postmodernist theory from Bataille, Foucault, Deleuze and Zizek, among others. The closing chapter views the lens of necrophilia through surrealism and pop art. Karolina Urbaniak's unsettling wax casts adorning each chapter add to the sensation of flesh that is cold and undergoing a metamorphosis of decay. A highly aesthetic and philosophical book, it is unique not only for its subject matter but as a psychoanalysis on sex, death and human desire.

THE LIGHTS and Other Stories
BY IBRAHIM R. INEKE. Illustrated by
the author. *Zagava*, 2023.

Dutch author and artist,
Ibrahim R. Ineke is well known for
his graphic novels and illustrative
work. While he is not translated
often into English, he is a highly
underrated practitioner of strange
tales and the weird.

Ineke's talent as a visual
narrator lends itself to his descrip-
tive eloquence. With stories set
primarily below sea level in the
Netherlands, a musty damp
pervades many of the tales, with heavy mists and dank claustro-
phobia. There is a vivid ease and sense of intimacy with his envi-
ronments, even when ascribing interiors with dream-like qualities,
from portals to mysterious entrance ways. The reader journeys into
a world of abandoned places, crumbling brutalist infrastructure
and further on into wild pantheistic landscapes.

Characters are fleshed out with unexpected humor, pathos and
vulnerability in the manner of Robert Aickman, Shirley Jackson
and Arthur Machen. We meet carefree children playing in the
forests unaware there is a liminal boundary. Aging detectives
unable to quit no matter how bizarre a case evolves. Themes of
class run throughout, as destitute artists contrast with their peers
feigning mock poverty, and working-class women are juxtaposed
against the spoils of wealth. Many of his narrators are isolated
both by the location they find themselves in and their sense of spiritual unease and disquietude. With an artist's eye for detail Ineke's
writing is beautifully crafted.

Contributors

Martin Cahill is an Ignyte Award-nominated author living just north of New York City. His novella, *Audition For The Fox*, will be published Fall 2025 by Tachyon Publications, and he was a recent contributor to *Critical Role: Vox Machina—Stories Untold*. He is a graduate of the Clarion Writers' Workshop of 2014 and his fiction can be found in Reactor, *Clarkesworld, Lightspeed Magazine*, and many other publications. His short story, "Godmeat," appeared in *The Best American Science Fiction and Fantasy 2019* anthology, and his non-fiction can be found at *Catapult, Ghostfire Gaming, Reactor*, and others. You can find him online at @mcflycahill90.

MK Cooper is a Chicago-based artist who has been working with acrylic paints for over 10 years. Their work focuses on dark themes, exploring concepts of mortality and the human experience through their paintings. https://www.instagram.com/bearded_artist_stu dios

Malcolm Devlin is the author of the novellas *And Then I Woke Up* and *Engines Beneath Us*; and the short story collections *You Will Grow Into Them*, and *Unexpected Places to Fall From*. He lives in Brisbane, Australia.

Shikhar Dixit has sold over forty short stories to such venues as *Weird Horror, Dark Regions, Strange Horizons, Not One of Us, The Darker Side* (ed. by John Pelan), *Songs From Dead Singers* (ed. by Michael Kelly) and two Barnes & Noble anthologies. Many of his stories have received Honorable Mention in various volumes of *The Year's Best Fantasy & Horror*, edited by Ellen Datlow and Terri Windling. He is also an illustrator for many of the same publications his fiction has appeared in. Shikhar is writing his first novel. He lives with his wife in the deep, dark heart of New Jersey.

Meg Elison is a Hugo, Philip K. Dick and Locus award winning author, as well as a Nebula, Sturgeon, and Otherwise awards finalist. A prolific short story writer and essayist, Elison has been published in *Scientific American, McSweeney's, Fantasy & Science Fiction, Fangoria,* and *Best American Science Fiction and Fantasy*. Elison is a high school dropout and a graduate of UC Berkeley. She lives in Brooklyn. megelison.com

Orrin Grey is a skeleton who likes monsters as well as the author of several spooky books. His stories of ghosts, monsters, and sometimes the ghosts of monsters can be found in dozens of anthologies, including Ellen Datlow's *Best Horror of the Year*. He resides in the suburbs of Kansas City and watches lots of scary movies. You can visit him online at orringrey.com

Vince Haig is an illustrator, designer, and author. You can visit Vince at his website: barquing.com

Françoise Harvey lives in North East England but grew up on an even smaller island. She has had stories published in *Bourbon Penn, Cast of Wonders, The Dark, Black Static, Interzone, Best British Short Stories 2017* and more, as well chapbook "Guest" published by Nightjar Press. She is host of local magazine NARC's *My Writing Life* podcast (which means she gets to interview other writers about how they write), is a part-time librarian and more-time musician. She's working on a novel.

John Patrick Higgins is a writer, illustrator, and filmmaker. His debut novel, *Fine,* was published by *Sagging Meniscus Press* in

November 2024, and the same company published his memoir, *Teeth: An Oral History*, in April 2024. A semi-sequel to *Teeth*, *Spine*, will be published in June 2025. He aims to catalogue each failing body part as it happens. He lives in Belfast and goes for long walks in the rain. He is working on a short fiction collection called *No Light in the Trees*.

Alexander James is a writer of weird fiction and poetry based in West London. You can find more of his work at alex-james.com/

Rebecca Kuder is the absolute mistress of her own body. Her books include *The Eight Mile Suspended Carnival* (What Books Press) and *Dear Inner Critic: a self-doubt activity book* (Literary Kitchen). Her shorter work has been published in *Los Angeles Review of Books; Hags on Fire; Bayou Magazine; Shadows and Tall Trees; Year's Best Weird Fiction; The Rumpus; Crooked Houses*; and elsewhere. She received an MFA from Antioch University LA and an individual artist excellence award from the Ohio Arts Council. Rebecca is also a writing coach. She lives in Yellow Springs, Ohio, with the writer Robert Freeman Wexler and their child. www.rebeccakuder.com

Spencer Nitkey is a writer of the weird, the wonderful, the horrible, and the (hopefully) beautiful. He lives in Philadelphia with his wife and a dog named after a French postmodernist. He was a finalist for the 2023 Eugie Foster Memorial Award for Short Fiction, and has been nominated for a Rhysling Award, Best Small Fictions, and Pushcart Prize. His writing has appeared, or is forthcoming, in *Apex Magazine, Diabolical Plots, Lightspeed Magazine, Weird Horror, Flash Fiction Online*, and others. You can find out more about him and read more of his stories on his website, spencernitkey.com

Lysette Stevenson is a stage manager with a rural outdoor equestrian theatre company and a second generation bookseller. She lives in British Columbia.

Simon Strantzas is the author of six collections of short fiction, including *Only the Living Are Lost* (Hippocampus Press, 2023), and editor of a number of anthologies, including *Year's Best Weird Fiction, Vol. 3*. Combined, he's been a finalist for four Shirley Jackson

Awards, two British Fantasy Awards, and the World Fantasy Award. His fiction has appeared in numerous annual best-of anthologies, and in venues such as *Nightmare*, *The Dark*, and *Cemetery Dance*. In 2014, his edited anthology, *Aickman's Heirs*, won the Shirley Jackson Award. He lives with his wife in Toronto, Canada.

Jocelyn Szczepaniak-Gillece teaches Film Studies at the University of Wisconsin-Milwaukee; her weird fiction appears or will appear in places like *Apocalypse Confidential*, *Exacting Clam*, *Sublunary Review*, *The Quarter(ly)*, and others. Her first novel, *Poltergeist*, is forthcoming with Apocalypse Confidential.

www.ingramcontent.com/pod-product-compliance
Lightning Source LLC
Chambersburg PA
CBHW050307260626
47156CB00005B/1703